CARIBBEAN CRUISE VACATION

By

PHILLIP G. ABBOTT

Copyright

EXT. PARKING LOT, STEPHENSON FOAM COMPANY-DAY

WILLIAMSBURG, KENTUCKY 5 PM

The sound and view of a factory whistle.

JAKE cranks his 1971 rusted out Ford pickup. Moves out of
the factory parking lot onto Hwy 92 South, southwest from
Williamsburg to Hurricane Hollow Road.

He turns on the radio.

                    JAKE
                (sings along)
          My name is John Lee Pettimore, just
          like my daddy and his daddy
          before.You could smell the whiskey
          burnin' down Copperhead Road.

JAKE moves fast down the two lane highway. No traffic.

An eight point buck stands in the left lane ahead. NO
traffic coming either way. JAKE slows the truck while
reaching for his rifle hanging in the rear window. He stops.
The buck is looking directly into the driver's side window
at JAKE. JAKE (slowly) moves the rifle down into position
while cocking the lever. He lays the rifle on the window
sill and aims square between the buck's eyes.

The buck charges the truck hitting the door with the large
horns. JAKE recoils discharging a round through his
windshield. Glass (flies).

The deer runs away.

A sheriff's patrol unit rolls up slowly and the sound of one
quick (REPORT)comes from the siren. He pulls up next to
JAKE'S window.

JAKE is scrambling to sit up. Glass all over him. The hood
of his truck and the pavement are covered with glass chards.

                    DEPUTY
          Howdy there Jake. What happened
          here?

                    JAKE
          Oh nothin'. I reckon a bird or rock
          flew into my windshield. I'll just
          get out and clean off the hood.

                    DEPUTY
          Nice rifle.

                    JAKE
          Thanks.

JAKE puts it back into the rear rack.

                    DEPUTY
          Seen any deer round these parts
          lately?

                    JAKE
          No sir. Reckon we'll have to wait
          till fall to see em'.

                    DEPUTY
          Yep. Have a good day .

The deputy pulls away slowly. JAKE brushes away some glass
fragments and drives away.

CUT TO

JAKE'S truck (ZOOMS) past newly leafing hardwoods over
rolling hills. Spring flowers just blooming. Pollen in the
air. Truck hangs right onto Happy Hollow then onto Hurricane
Hollow. His driveway on right ahead. Gravel covered. He
turns in slowly.Cuts engine. Red Bone hound approaches
(BARKING). Climbs up into cab with Jake.

                    JAKE
          Hey Maynard ole buddy. Where's your
          momma?

JAKE jumps down out of truck .JAKE turns to look at the
dents on his door and broken windshield . He strolls up to
the deck in front of double wide trailer. Opens door.

INT. TRAILER - DAY

JAKE enters the double wide trailer. Supper is on the table.
NADINE places the cornbread on the table.

                    NADINE
          Hi baby, alright kids let's eat.

                    JAKE
          Hi baby.

JJ and JENELLA sit with JAKE and NADINE at the table.

                                              (CONTINUED)

                    JAKE (cont'd)
          JJ, say grace.

                    JJ
          Dear lord, thank you for this day
          and our many blessings.

The cat, RUFUS, jumps onto the table and licks milk out of
JAKE'S glass. JJ raises his eyelids and sees the cat.

                    JJ (cont'd)
          And a special prayer for Rufus, who
          is the best cat in the world and
          should be treated kindly all the
          time.

JAKE looks up at JJ and notices the cat licking his milk.

                    JJ (cont'd)
          Amen.

JAKE raises his hand to the cat. JJ looks at him. JAKE
gently lifts the cat off the table.

                    JAKE
          Rufus, today is your lucky day.

                    JJ
          Daddy, what are we going to do this
          summer for a real vacation when
          school's out?

                    JAKE
          Don't know yet boy. Just keep your
          pants on and we will think of
          somethin' good.

JAKE'S seventeen year old daughter.

                    JENELLA
          Yea daddy.I don't wanna start hair
          stylin' school this fall and tell
          everybody I didn't do nothin' this
          summer.

                    JAKE
          Hang on there baby girl. Daddy's
          gonna make ya happy. You just wait.

                    NADINE
          Let's eat y'all.Your daddy worked
          hard this week. He thinks better on
          a full stomach.

INT. TRAILER - LIGHTS OUT MIDNIGHT

JAKE lying in bed staring at ceiling. Crickets and Katy Dids (ECHO) up the hollow.

INT. TRAILER - MORNING 7 AM

JAKE wakes, rises and stretches. NADINE rolls over.

He slides his feet down the hallway in boxers and sleeveless tee shirt. John Deere hat pushed down on his head.He reaches for a cup in the kitchen. Pours a cup of coffee and heads out the front door.

EXT. TRAILER FRONT DECK - MORNING

JAKE stands on (WOBBLY) deck. Takes a sip of coffee. MAYNARD under the deck wakes. Tail wagging across bottom step tread. JAKE steps down onto Maynard's tail. The dog lurches from under the porch (HOWLING). JAKE spins around. Coffee cup flies up. JAKE hits the ground on his back. MAYNARD approaches and licks him generously in the face.

                    JAKE
          Get away dang it!

JAKE rolls over and gets up slowly. Dusting off his rear , he heads down the driveway to the mailbox. Opens the box and retrieves a stack of mail.

                    JAKE (cont'd)
          Same ole'stuff.

JAKE moves up the driveway thumbing through the mail. He spots a brochure, LOW BUDGET CARIBBEAN CRUISE VACATION. He notices MAYNARD cowling under the deck.

                    JAKE (cont'd)
          Sorry ole' buddy. Is your tail OK.

MAYNARD wags his tail and sets his jaws down onto the cool earth. JAKE climbs the steps and goes inside.

                              INTERIOR TRAILER

NADINE enters the kitchen .

                    NADINE
          What in the world happened out
          there? Is Maynard alright?

(CONTINUED)

                         JAKE
              Yea, he just got his tail in a
              bind. Hey look here honey. I found
              us a real cruise vacation we can
              afford.The kids are gonna love it.

NADINE leans over and takes the brochure. She sits down with
JAKE on the couch.

                         JAKE (cont'd)
              I know what you are thinkin' honey,
              but I want to show you somethin'.
              Come here.

He takes her hand. Leads her to the kitchen window over the
sink. JAKE points out to the backyard. An orange mini school
bus sits full of aluminum cans and Marlboro packs. A cow is
eating weeds next to the bus.

                         JAKE (cont'd)
              Right there darlin' is our ticket.
              I will clean her out and sell off
              all the cans and trade for all
              those empty packs. We have enough
              cash to make up the difference. All
              you got to do is say yes.

                         NADINE
              Jake, that cruise is plenty cheap
              enough, but do you realize we have
              to drive plumb to Mobile, Alabama?

                         JAKE
              Honey, I can have that bus runnin'
              in no time at all. Just think, we
              are on a big cruise boat sailing
              off to some island paradise. Come
              on baby. Let's do it.

NADINE hesitates for a moment.She is looking at JAKE.

                         NADINE
              OK.

                         JAKE
              What?

                         NADINE
              I said OK.

JAKE stares into her eyes for a second.

                         JAKE
               Go wake the kids! I'll wake the
               kids!

INT. JENIFER COUTREAU'S BUNGALOW - DAY

LOS ANGELES , CALIFORNIA

The telephone rings . A beautiful fair complexioned woman in
her late twenties answers wearing only a bathrobe and towel
wrapped around her head.

                         JENIFER
               Hello.

An aspiring businessman on the other end.

                         TRISTAN
               Hi babe. What are you doing?

                         JENIFER
               Just out of the shower honey. Where
               are you?

                         TRISTAN
               Working of course. Do you want to
               meet for lunch around noon?

                         JENIFER
               Sure. Where?

                         TRISTAN
               Capella's OK.

                         JENIFER
               Fine.

TRISTAN holds the phone away from his ear and looks down for
a second. He puts it back to his ear.

                         TRISTAN
               Look honey, I am going to be sent
               to London for a conference in a few
               days. I'll be gone for a couple of
               weeks. Career move up. You know.
               Can we reschedule the cruise to
               Hawaii for later ?
                    (STUNNED SILENCE)

                         JENIFER
               You're kidding?

                         TRISTAN
          I have to be there. It is a crucial
          career move. It can't be canceled.

                         JENIFER
          Tristan, we planned this trip a
          year ago. You always push it back.
          Now again. No more. Not this time.

                         TRISTAN
          Don't do this now. That stupid
          cruise can wait a few more weeks.
          It makes no sense . We can schedule
          it when I return. Promise.

                         JENIFER
          I have waited for everything. Put
          my career on hold. My life on hold
          for God's sakes. We are doing this
          now.

                         TRISTAN
          I can't change everything around
          right now. What are you doing to
          me?

JENNY drops the phone. She runs to her bedroom and launches
onto it with tears streaming. Her makeup a mess. She cries
(LOUDLY). Wipes her face. Smears the makeup. Gets up and
walks straight back to the phone on the floor. Picks it up
and slams in down on the receiver. She picks it back up
holding it to her ear.

                         JENIFER
          Goodbye Tristan. I don't like your
          name anyway.

She drops the phone. Tears streaming, makeup running, she
turns and heads straight for her PC desk. Wipes her eyes.
Black eye shadow streaking down her face. She races through
favorites on her computer and finds several.

                         JENIFER (cont'd)
          This one. No. That one. Here it is.

The PC mouse moves quickly. Click. Click. Screen shows LOW
BUDGET CARIBBEAN CRUISE VACATION. JENNY scrolls down,hits
pay here. Pay Pal transaction is completed.

                         JENIFER (cont'd)
          Done. I'm gone.

INT. MERRILL LYNCH OFFICES MANHATTAN - DAY

NEW YORK, NEW YORK

BEN is sitting at his desktop running through numbers. He is
holding his cell phone between his shoulder and ear.

                    BEN
          Yes sir, that account is solid and
          I will process your request
          immediately. As a matter of fact, I
          am doing that now. (Pause) You too.
          Have a good day.

In one motion, he releases the shoulder grip on the cell and
catches it with his left hand. BEN continues to blaze away
on the PC. His cell rings. He answers.

                    BEN
          Hello.

(other end)

                    PRISCILLA
          Hello Darling. I can't make the
          noon lunch. Hair appointment. Wish
          you were here.

                    BEN
          And where is that?

                    PRISCILLA
          I'm home on my way out.

(PRISCILLA IS IN BED WITH HER LOVER)

                    BEN
          OK, when can I see you?

                    PRISCILLA
          Oh, is six good for you at Le
          Bernardin downtown? I'll call in.

                    BEN
          Sure, fine. I got to go, lots to
          do. See you there.

                    PRISCILLA
          Kisses darling.

PRISCILLA snaps the razor phone shut and drops it on the
bed as she reaches out for her lover.

(CONTINUED)

                         PRISCILLA (cont'd)
              He is such a sweet boy and makes
              great money too. Look sweetheart, I
              need to go.

BEN goes for coffee at the common station and meets a friend
in the office.

                         BEN
              Hey man, what's up?

                         CARTER
              Busy, very busy. Hey, what are you
              doing tonight?

                         BEN
              Meeting Priscilla for dinner. Why?

                         CARTER
              I thought she was seeing someone
              else. You two still an item?

Ben turns toward Carter (Pauses)

                         BEN
              Seeing someone else? Who told you
              that?

                         CARTER
                   (Fumbling with words)
              Nobody. Maybe I misunderstood.
              Could be someone else. Gotta go
              buddy. See ya.

BEN'S eyes follow CARTER out of the room. BEN returns to his
desk. The section manager walks up holding a brochure and
envelope.

                         ROBERT
              Hey Ben, take this and use it. You
              deserve it. Get out of here and get
              some overdue rest. Come back
              smiling.

ROBERT hands the envelope and brochure to BEN.

                         BEN
              What is that?

                         ROBERT
              You'll see.

ROBERT walks away. BEN opens the envelope containing tickets for a cruise. Ben tosses the brochure on his desk with the tickets. He leans back in his chair interlocking his fingers behind his head.

INT. LE BERNARDIN - NIGHT

BEN stands near the Maitre De waiting.PRISCILLA enters the restaurant smiling. They are escorted to a table and seated.

                    PRISCILLA
          How was your day darling?

                    BEN
          Probably not as good as yours, but
          OK.How was yours?

                    PRISCILLA
          Very good thank you.

PRISCILLA leans toward BEN and whispers softly.
                    (continues)
          Sweetheart, your fly is open.

Without looking down, BEN reaches and closes his fly.

                    BEN
          What would you like for an
          appetizer?

                    PRISCILLA
          Why you of course dear.

PRISCILLA tilts her head and unrolls her linen napkin.

                    BEN
          Are you sure?

PRISCILLA locks her eyes on BEN.

                    PRISCILLA
          Yes. Why do you say that? You know
          I love you .

BEN looks around the room and back into her eyes.

                    BEN
          Of course. Would you like to order
          now.

                         PRISCILLA
               Ben, you look distracted. Tell me
               what is wrong.

BEN hesitates.

                         BEN
               If there is someone else just tell
               me. I can handle it.

                         PRISCILLA
               Has some young thing in your office
               been whispering in your ear?

                         BEN
               No. What does that mean.

                         PRISCILLA
               You know, Ben, pretty young
               associates looking for a good man
               with a bright future could be
               deceiving you with lies about me.

                         BEN
               Come on. Maybe pretty young men are
               whispering in your ear. Give me a
               break here.

PRISCILLA sits silent for a moment head down.
                    (BEN continues)
               It is true. You are seeing someone
               else! Oh my God!

Priscilla looks up and is blushing. People nearby turn to
see what is happening.

                         PRISCILLA
               Just calm down for a moment. I can
               explain.It is a jungle out there. A
               girl has to consider all her
               options. Please don't take it
               personally.

                         BEN
               I won't if you don't take this
               personally. I'm gone!

BEN rises quickly from his chair.His thighs push against the
round pedestal dining table tilting it over sharply into
PRISCILLA'S lap. The linen tablecloth is caught in BEN'S
fly. Silverware, dishes and water glasses pour onto
PRISCILLA. She is pinned to her chair by the table in her
lap. BEN reaches for the tablecloth and yanks hard to

release it from his crotch. It is stuck. He walks away
dragging the tablecloth while yanking on it as he goes. It
releases from his fly as he passes the Maitre De. He throws
it at the Maitre De and exits the building.

EXT. BEAUREGARD MANSION , HOUSTON TEXAS - MORNING

Warm morning air with clear blue skies. JOHN and MADDIE sit
sipping coffee and reading on the pool patio. JOHN drops the
Wall Street Journal and looks at MADDIE reading a fashion
magazine.

                    JOHN
          You know, I was thinking. We have
          done just about everything there is
          to do and have everything anyone
          could ask for. What would you like
          to do next?

MADDIE is focused on her reading. She looks over her
magazine and lowers her sunglasses exposing her blue eyes.

                    MADDIE
          What did you say dear?

                    JOHN
          You weren't listening. What do you
          want to do?

                    MADDIE
          Sugar, we are doing something. Look
          around. What else could you
          possibly want to do?

JOHN gets up slowly. His bathing trunks sagging around his
waist. He walks toward the crystal clear lap pool.

                    JOHN
          I am just plain bored.

MADDIE lays her magazine down and gets up. She follows JOHN
to poolside. They sit (SWISHING) their feet in the cool
water. MADDIE looks over at JOHN.

                    MADDIE
          Listen ole' boy. You know I would
          follow you anywhere, but we have so
          much going on in Houston with the
          charities and functions, it keeps
          me tied up days on end. If you are
          bored, it is not from lack of
          something to do. What is on your
          mind?

The terrace doors open behind them and KATE moves across the
patio stones toward them. She is a lovely, athletic woman. A
natural glow accompanies her as she approaches her parents.

                    KATE
          Hey, what are you two doing? I
          can't leave you alone for a minute
          without you pawing all over each
          other like two puppies.

Both JOHN and MADDIE turn to see their daughter as she
glides across the patio.

                    JOHN
          Baby girl. Where have you been?
          That graduate school stuff is
          keeping you from us too much. Come
          here.

KATE bends over and kisses his forehead. She turns and
kisses her mother on the cheek.

                    MADDIE
          Your poor daddy is bored to tears.
          He needs you to get him going and
          fast. If anyone can do that it is
          you dear one.

                    KATE
          Is that right daddy? What is it,
          don't you like to ride your horses
          anymore? I know, you miss the oil
          and grit on your hands and face
          from all those gushers you tackled
          back in the day. Come on let's go
          for a swim.

KATE pushes JOHN into the pool and joins him. Floating
together she looks at him directly.

                    KATE
          Daddy, I have been wanting to go
          diving again. We are researching
          coral reef problems and I think you
          and mom would enjoy some salt air.

                    JOHN
          I am in water right now and there
          is salt in the kitchen. Why would I
          want to do that?

                    KATE
          OK. What if I told you it was for a
          potential investment opportunity? I
          have been looking at low priced
          cruise trips. Some of these
          entrepreneurs are breaking into the
          market with barefoot cruises using
          smaller ships. I get to dive and
          you get to help me decide if small
          cruise ships are the new wave. What
          do you say?

JOHN smiles at his daughter.

                    JOHN
          Would that make you happy?

                    KATE
          Yes. You and mom will really enjoy
          it.

JOHN looks at MADDIE.

                    JOHN
          What do you think honey?

                    MADDIE
          Oh, why not, as long as the ship is
          nice and we are not gone too long?

INT. BAY SHORE DIE MAKERS LTD. - DAY

MOBILE, ALABAMA

MATT is leaned over a bench making adjustments on a new die
he built. His hands are greasy. Someone walks up from
behind.

                    WORKER
          Matt, you have a call in the
          office.

Without looking up MATT keeps working.

                    MATT
          OK. Thanks.

MATT grabs a rag and wipes his hands as he turns to go to
the office phone. The machine shop is (LOUD).

He enters the office door and shuts it behind him. (SHOP
NOISE DIMINISHES). Matt answers the phone. He is looking
through a plate glass window separating the shop from the
office.

                    MATT
          Hello. (PAUSE) Yes. OK great. When
          can I pick it up.(PAUSE). I will be
          there. Thanks.

MATT reaches for his cell and speed dials his uncle MIKE.
MATT turns to look at the work board on the wall.

                    MATT (cont'd)
          Hey Mike, can you stop by
          Major's Electronics and pick
          up the GPS package?

                    MIKE
          Sure, how is everything else going?
          Do you think we can move Bertha
          this weekend?

                    MATT
          Yes. she is ready. If you can round
          everybody up this weekend, we will
          drill the crew. I need to see the
          banker tomorrow. Oh. did the fuel
          stock arrive?

                    MIKE
          Yea. She is loaded. Are you excited
          yet?

                    MATT
          After three years, you bet and I
          appreciate you sticking with me .
          If dad was here he would be mighty
          proud.

                    MIKE
          No problem young man. See you
          tomorrow. Bye.

MATT hangs up the phone while looking through the plate
glass window separating the shop from the office.

INT MOBILE CITIZENS BANK, MOBILE, AL. - 2PM

MATT strides into the bank entrance and down the hallway to his left. He approaches an office door. He knocks (LIGHTLY). MILFORD GRAY opens the office door.

                    MILFORD
          Come in.

                    MATT
          Thanks. How are you?

                    MILFORD
          Good thank you.

MATT eases into the office and sits in front of MILFORD'S desk. MILFORD sits down and slides his bifocals on smoothly as he opens a file. He looks up at MATT.

                    MILFORD (cont'd)
          We need to discuss your loan so
          that you will be aware of the
          details . We have packaged the loan
          to include past due interest
          payments as well as credit for
          payments made to interest and
          principal over the last period.

MILFORD shows MATT the file details. MATT leans forward glancing down as MILFORD moves his index finger across the paper.

                    MATT
          Yes sir.

                    MILFORD
          According to our records, you have
          invested $100,000 cash and $57,000
          more in cash from you uncle. We
          have loaned out $350,000 for the
          project. Your intensive labor
          invested counts for some value
          which could be interpreted as sweat
          equity. Would you agree that Bertha
          could be said to be valued at
          $500,000 at this time?

                    MATT
          Yes sir, if not a lot more.

                    MILFORD
          Alright then, the repayment of the
          principal amount $350,000 will
                    (MORE)

                         MILFORD (cont'd)
              start with your receipts for
              passenger fares received to date.
              This should catch us up on the late
              interest payments. Is that
              satisfactory?

                         MATT
              That'll work.

MILFORD leans back and takes off his glasses.

                         MILFORD
              MATTHEW your father was a hard
              working man and honest. I think you
              are just like him. Good luck on
              your first cruise. I will be seeing
              you when you return.

                         MATT
              Thanks. See you later.

Both men rise. Shake hands. MATT leaves.

EXT. MOBILE CHANNEL - AFTERNOON

BLACK BAYOU INLET

MATT drives up Hwy 43 outside Mobile in his pickup truck. It
is late afternoon. He pulls off the road onto a dirt road
leading to Bertha's mooring site. He climbs out of the truck
and goes aboard the boat. He enters the captains bridge
carrying components for the GPS package. Mike is on the
bridge working on other things.

                         MATT
              Hey buddy.

                         MIKE
              Hey, look. I built this special for
              Frank. I call it his perch pad.
              What do you think?

MIKE holds a metal padded seat with fasteners.

                         MATT
              It looks good to me. Why don't you
              put it right next to the wheel,
              that way he can keep an eye on the
              horizon for us?

                                                         (CONTINUED)

                         MIKE
               Consider it done my friend.

MIKE places the seat on the bridge console while MATT
adjusts the components for the GPS package. MATT finishes
snapping the assembly together and inserting the final
components as he looks over at MIKE.

                         MATT
               That is it. We are now ready to
               cruise.. Fire her up while I go
               down and cast off the lines. We can
               move her down the channel to port
               tonight.

MATT leaves the bridge going down steel steps and railing
hopping off the last step onto the deck. He casts off two
large ropes tying Bertha to the dock and reaches for his
Nextel. MATT raises the Nextel to his face.

                         MATT (cont'd)
               Let's move out.Easy now.

Bertha moves back and eases out into the channel. MATT calls
out movements to MIKE steering the boat on the bridge.

EXT. OVERHEAD SHOT MOBILE CHANNEL GEOGRAPHY - SUNDOWN

Bertha moves slowly down the channel toward Mobile. Camera
pans down river with Bertha's profile in view.

INT. BERTHA'S BRIDGE - SUNDOWN

Deep sound of powerful engines. MATT is at the wheel. He
looks at MIKE sitting beside him.

                         MATT
               Listen to her sing to us.

                         MIKE
               Yea.

MATT and MIKE are looking through the forward window
downstream.

                         MATT
               Kinda like just getting married.
               You're scared but you love it!

                                                    (CONTINUED)

                         MIKE
           Are you kidding? You are married.
           (Pause). To Bertha.

                         MATT
           I reckon. At least for now. Do you
           want to get married again?

                         MIKE
           No. I had the best woman on earth.
           I hope she is out there watching
           this right now.

                         MATT
           You know she is.

EXT. WILLIAMSBURG KY. JAKE'S HOUSE -DAY

Yellow mini bus sitting in driveway loaded for the trip. On
the side, a graphic HOME SKOOLED. JAKE is on top loading
baggage. NADINE exits the trailer with more stuff. She looks
up at JAKE.

                         JAKE
           Baby, that's all we can take. Did
           you think we were movin' to Mobile?

                         NADINE
           I reckon this is it. Do you want
           that bag of Cheetos, because you
           ain't gettin' those pickled eggs?

                         JAKE
           No. Let's get goin'. Tell the kids
           we're ready.

Trailer door is open. NADINE turns toward the door.

                         NADINE
           Are y'all goin' with us or not?
           Come on. Get some water and food
           for Maynard. Fill that five gallon
           bucket up under the shed. Nellie
           Caldwell will come by tomorrow to
           check on him.

JAKE climbs down off the bus and approaches NADINE.

                         JAKE
           I gotta go next door and see the
           old man. Be right back.

JAKE moves across the front yard and walks through a small
thicket with pines to WILSON'S small frame house. WILSON is
sitting in his rocking chair on the front porch half asleep.
Shotgun leaning against the wall behind him. Chickens poking
around the yard and on the porch. JAKE moves next to the
side of the house.

                    JAKE (cont'd)
          Mr. Wilson are you there?

No answer. Just the chickens cackling.

                    JAKE (cont'd)
          Mr. Wilson. (LOUDER)

Nothing. Jake eases around the corner of the house to the
front porch. He stands in front of the old man.

                    JAKE (cont'd)
          Mr. Wilson.

WILSON'S eyes fly open . His straw hat pushed down over his
eyes. His right arm moves over the rocker arm. He reaches
for the shotgun knocking it over onto the porch floor. The
gun discharges blowing a chicken into feathers. JAKE stands
(FROZEN). WILSON looks up at him.

                    JAKE (cont'd)
          I just came by to ask you if you
          would check the mail. We will be
          gone for a few days.

                    WILSON
          Well, you can just go to hell too.
          Look what you did.

JAKE stares at WILSON and hesitates. WILSON'S foggy gray
eyes (GLARING). WILSON spits a chew of tobacco onto the
porch.

                    JAKE
          That's OK, never mind. You have a
          good day now. Nice to see ya.

JAKE backs away slowly and eases over to the side of the
house and disappears into the woods.

NADINE is standing at the trailer front door with keys in
hand. She locks the door and turns to see JAKE crossing the
yard back to the house.

                         NADINE
               What in the world is that old man
               doin' now?

                         JAKE
               Nothin', let's go.

JJ and JENELLA are in the bus waiting. JAKE and NADINE get
in. JAKE starts the engine. It backfires and smokes. He
backs out and gases it.

The mini bus is moving along up Hurricane Hollow road. JJ
sees the eight point buck standing along the side of the
road looking at the mini bus.

                         JJ
               Look daddy, ain't that the buck you
               been after for a couple of years?

                         JAKE
               Yea boy, I'll get him in the fall.

View of the mini bus (ZOOMING) past the deer.

EXT. ATLANTA, I-75 INTERSTATE - DAY

TRAFFIC JAM DOWNTOWN

The mini bus is sitting in six lanes of stopped traffic.
Jake puts his tattooed arm out the driver's side window.
NADINE is fanning her brow with a magazine. JJ and JENELLA
are sleeping. JAKE looks over and notices a BMW . The driver
is staring at the bus. JAKE raises his hand. The BMW moves
forward.

                         NADINE
               Can you believe this traffic?

                         JAKE
               Never seen so many cars in one
               spot.

                         NADINE
               Get us out of here Jake.

                         JAKE
               Are you kiddin' darlin. Ain't no
               way.

NADINE points to the emergency lane. It is blocked by two
lanes of traffic to the right. JAKE looks at NADINE
                    (CONTINUES)
                         (MORE)

                                               (CONTINUED)

                         JAKE (cont'd)
          You really want me to do that?

                         NADINE
          Do it now or I will.

                         JAKE
          Hang on.

JAKE forces his way over in front of two cars to his right
and moves into the emergency lane. (HORNS BLASTING). The
mini bus speeds down the emergency lane passing cars for a
quarter mile until JAKE finds an opening and weaves his way
through past the stopped traffic behind him. The mini bus
flies down the interstate.

INT. MOBILE INTERNATIONAL AIRPORT - DAY

JENNY walks quickly through the airport terminal to baggage
claim circular. She retrieves her rolling baggage and has
one carry on over her shoulder. She exits the terminal and
waits for a cab.

BEN is standing near a cab stand with his luggage. He spots
a cab to his right a few yards away. JENNY sees the same cab
straight in front of her. She moves quickly toward the cab
losing a shoe in the process. She is waving her hand and
(SHOUTING) to the cabby. BEN moves to his right and reaches
the cab before JENNY. The cabby stands behind the cab and
sees both racing toward him.

                         BEN
          Hey , can you open the trunk for me
          please?

                         CABBY
          Sure.

CABBY opens the trunk. BEN starts throwing his luggage in.

JENNY is standing beside him.
                    (to BEN)

                         JENNY
          Did you not see me standing here
          first? How rude.

                         BEN
          Oh. I guess I didn't.

                         JENNY
               Well?

                          BEN
               Well what?

Cabby interrupts.

                         CABBY
               Look folks. One of you is going to
               have to decide pretty quick here.
               We have to be moving soon.

BEN looks down and sees JENNY wearing only one shoe.

                          BEN
               Where are you going?

                         JENNY
               Cruise Terminal.

                          BEN
               Me too. Why don't we share the
               ride?

                         JENNY
               OK.

                          BEN
               Let me get your shoe while you load
               your luggage.

BEN walks away to retrieve her shoe. Cabby loads her
luggage. Both enter the cab. Cab pulls away.

EXT. PRIVATE HANGAR , MOBILE INT. AIRPORT

The BEAUREGARDS step down off the Lear jet. JOHN follows .
He trips down a step pushing MADDY into KATE. The pilot is
standing in front of KATE. She falls into the pilot knocking
him down on the concrete tarmac. He is unconscious.

JOHN walks past the pilot.

                         JOHN
               Nice flight.

JOHN looks around.

                    JOHN (cont'd)
               Could someone please help this man?

The BEAUREGARDS walk toward a waiting limousine. Baggage is being loaded for them.

EXT. CRUISE TERMINAL PARKING , WATER STREET - DAY

MOBILE, ALABAMA

The orange mini bus is stopped at the parking gate shack. Jake is looking at the attendant. Inside the bus, NADINE is sweating. JJ and JENELLA are arguing.

                    JAKE
          This ain't no recreational vehicle
          or RV as you say.

                    ATTENDANT
          Sir, once again, please move your
          RV out of this lot and turn around.
          The RV lot is over there.

ATTENDANT points toward RV lot.

                    JAKE
          Do you realize it costs a hundred
          bucks a week over there? Once
          again, I say this is a SUV not a
          RV.

                    ATTENDANT
          Sir, if you do not move this
          vehicle now, I will call the Port
          Authority and have it removed. You
          are holding up traffic.

JAKE folds his arms .

                    JAKE
          I'm stayin' right here till you let
          us in. Go ahead and call the law.

                    ATTENDANT
          Sir, I am going to let you pass
          this time, but you will have to pay
          at least half the cost of parking
          for an RV.

                    JAKE
          Fair enough.

The mini bus pulls forward. Behind the bus is an AMC Pacer with JUST MARRIED written on the rear window. A Tennessee license tag on the rear.

                                        (CONTINUED)

JAKE parks. The family exits the bus. They gather at the
rear of the bus. JAKE climbs up to retrieve the luggage and
bags and other assorted items in plastic bags.

                    JAKE (cont'd)
          Alright kids we are here. Let's
          grab everything and move out. Don't
          want to be late. Which way to the
          terminal Nadine?

NADINE surveys the port area and sees Port Entry Terminal 3.
She points toward the sign.

                    NADINE
          Right there. We have to go.

EXT. PORT TERMINAL 3 -DAY

A white limo pulls up to curbside. The BEAUREGARDS exit the
vehicle while the driver unloads baggage. A handler
approaches to carry the baggage. JOHN takes MADDIE by the
hand as KATE looks around.

                    JOHN
          Have you been to Mobile before
          dear?

                    MADDIE
          No . I always thought it was one of
          your portfolio stocks.

                    KATE
          Come on Mom.

The BEAUREGARDS walk toward the terminal concourse as BEN
AND JENNY arrive in the cab. They exit and grab their bags.
BEN and JENNY walk together to the terminal.

INT. CRUISE TERMINAL 3 - LATE AFTERNOON

Large crowd of people processing through the terminal gates.
The intercom departure times are announced.

                    INTERCOM
          Passengers sailing aboard the SS
          Bertha for Key West/St.Thomas
          cruise should be preparing for
          embarkation in 15 minutes. Please
          follow the purser agent's
          direction. Thank you.

People begin to assemble in the terminal and migrate toward
the exit gate onto the pier walkway. The appearance of
"country folk" is prominent . JAKE and family are moving
along together.

                    JAKE
          Why are so many people looking at
          us funny darlin'?

NADINE glances around the crowd.

                    NADINE
          I don't know baby. Maybe they
          recognize us. I don't remember
          meetin' any of them before. Do you?

                    JAKE
          No. I think they look strange with
          all those hearin' aids and talking
          to theirselves like that.

                    NADINE
          Reckon they come out here to get
          some fresh air and try to heal up a
          little. All that city noise
          probably ruined their hearin'.

                    JAKE
          Yea. Strange ain't it. I'm glad we
          live in the sticks.

BEN walks out onto the port decking and looks up at a large
cruise ship. JENNY stops to answer her cell phone as BEN
moves ahead.

                    JENNY
          Hello.
               (other end)

                    TRISTAN
          Jenny, don't hang up. I just wanted
          to tell you I can't stop thinking
          about us. I haven't slept since we
          last talked.

                    JENNY
          Tristan, don't even go there. Where
          are you?

                    TRISTAN
          Flying in from London. I will take
          a red eye flight tonight for LA.
          Will you be there?

                                        (CONTINUED)

                         JENNY
               Not exactly.

                         TRISTAN
               What's that supposed to mean? I
               need to see you and talk this thing
               out once and for all. Please, let
               me see you.

                         JENNY
               Tell you what. You keep talking and
               I will listen, but don't ask me any
               questions. OK, go ahead.

JENNY tosses the cell phone into Mobile bay as the
BEAUREGARDS observe the diversity of the crowd. MADDIE turns
to JOHN.

                         MADDIE
               John Beauregard, where are you
               taking me? These people look like
               the cast of the Beverly
               Hillbillies.

                         JOHN
               On a cruise dear.

Kate strolls along then looks back at her parents.

                         KATE
               Come on you two. Quit Lallygagging.

EXT. BERTHA - EVENING

DOCKSIDE

Captain MATTHEW DOBSON stands at the gangway with first
officer, MIKE TURNBUCKLE. MATT (SQUINTS) his eyes and points
forward.

                         MATT
               Here they come, Mike.

                         MIKE
               You got that right.

Behind them stands BERTHA. Two hundred fifty feet from stern
to bow. She is dwarfed by nearby cruise ships. BERTHA has
twin vertical exhausts rising twenty feet above deck. The
cabin superstructure is three stories tall with a wedge
shape in the forward area. The bridge sits forward of the V
shape structure. The Alabama state flag flies on the top
deck.

                                            (CONTINUED)

MATT turns around and looks up at BERTHA. He directs his
attention to the crew on board.

                    MATT
          Prepare for the guest's arrival. We
          are boarding passengers in five
          minutes.

A flurry of activity aboard. Crew members position for
passenger reception. The Activities coordinator walks down
the gangway with a loud speaker.

In the galley, cooks are preparing large amounts of
chicken,gravy, potatoes and salad.

One hundred fifty passengers gather nearby for boarding.MATT
looks at MIKE.

                    MATT (cont'd)
          OK, here we go. You ready? Tell the
          AC to use that bullhorn.

Activities Coordinator raises loudspeaker.

                    DAVID
          Welcome everyone. Please observe
          caution while climbing the gangway.
          Your captain, Matthew Dobson would
          like to greet everyone as they come
          aboard.We will direct you to your
          cabins as you come aboard BERTHA.

In the middle of the crowd John and Maddie look on and
listen. Maddie turns to John.

                    MADDIE
          Get me out of here right now.

                    JOHN
          Maddie, this is a low budget
          barefoot cruise. It may have
          venture potential for Kate. She
          seems happy to be here with us.
          Please, let's try this. If you
          don't like it we can fly home when
          we port at Key West. Deal?

                    MADDIE
          Oh, I suppose, but you promise to
          leave at Key West if things go bad,
          right?

                                            (CONTINUED)

                    JOHN
          That's the deal.

As the line forms in front of the gangway, KATE approaches
MATT. She reaches for his hand and smiles.

                    KATE
          Hello. I am Kate Beauregard.

MATT locks onto her eyes.

                    MATT
          Hello. (pause) Welcome aboard. I am
          Matt Dobson.

MATT is silenced by KATE'S beauty.

                    KATE
          Nice to meet you. Do you own this
          ship?

                    MATT
              (stutters slightly)
          UH. Yes. You're mine. I mean she is
          mine. Yes.

KATE slides by and other passengers follow. JAKE stands in
front of MATT.

                    JAKE
          Captain sir, This is a fine boat
          you got. Where is the dinin' hall?

                    MATT
          Just follow the crowd. The
          Activities Coordinator will show
          you. Welcome aboard.

Movement of the passengers going aboard BERTHA. Last
passengers accounted for. MATT and MIKE follow and ascend to
the bridge. Crewmen are busy on deck with preparations for
sailing. Some passengers stroll around the deck.

INT. BRIDGE - LATER

MATT is checking systems. MIKE is on radio to the engine
room.

                    MIKE
          Everything good down there. Give me
          status please. Over.

                                              (CONTINUED)

                    ENGINE ROOM CHIEF
          It's all go. Over.

                    MIKE
          Roger. Out.

EXT. ONBOARD BERTHA . LATE DAY SUNSET

Passengers milling about on deck.

MATT is on the bridge.

ON INTERCOM

                    MATT
          We will be leaving port in a few
          minutes. Please enjoy the sunset as
          we move out to sea. As a cautionary
          measure all deck chairs are secured
          to the deck. Please remain seated
          when acceleration of the ship
          begins. Bertha is built for speed
          and comfort. Thank you.

Some of the passengers standing against the stern railing
look down the side and notice large metallic fins on each
side of the ship just below the water line.

                    PASSENGER I
          Did you see those fins?

                    PASSENGER II
          What about that. This must be some
          kind of prototype hydrofoil .

Dock personnel are looking up at BERTHA.

                    DOCK WORKER
               (to co worker)
          Look at that thing. Can you believe
          those people actually boarded it.
          You talk about a redneck cruise,
          that's it.

INT. BERTHA - SUNSET

MATT steers BERTHA out of port toward Mobile Bay. He eases
her into the bay. Engines (RUMBLING)deep within the hull.

                         MATT
              I am throttling up a little.

BERTHA passes Dauphin Island and enters open sea. MATT
reaches for the intercom handset and turns it on.

                         MATT (cont'd)
              Please be seated. Thank you.

BERTHA moves across the smooth sea and begins to accelerate
rapidly. The bow rises gently as the stern is lowered
slightly. The large fins on the stern side of the hull move
to give lift to the ship.

JAKE SPARKS stands at a urinal in the common area men's room
on the deck. A row of men stand on either side of JAKE. Two
toilet stalls face two others on each end of the bathroom.
They are occupied. The bathroom floor is (TILTED). JAKE puts
his weight on his left foot. His right hand pushes against
the man next to him. On his left, men are sliding downhill.
The stall occupants on his right are (THROWN) off the toilet
seats and into the stall doors. On his left, occupants of
the two stalls are (PRESSED) against the toilet tanks.

BEN is sitting on the aft deck in a chair with drink in
hand. He is looking at the (ROLLING) wake created by BERTHA.
JENNY is walking around the cabin structure wall on the aft
deck. She approaches BEN from the rear. She falls forward
spilling her drink onto BEN'S head. JENNY falls over BEN and
into his lap head first. She is upside down between his
legs. Her feet in the air. BEN holds her (TIGHTLY).

NEWLYWED COUPLE from Tennessee is sitting on the fore deck
facing the sea. The force of the wind and acceleration
(PRESSES) them against the superstructure wall. Their faces
(TWISTED).

Man and wife in dining hall sit facing each other. They are
sipping drinks through straws as fast as possible. The angle
of their drinks (TILTED).

EXT. BERTHA - SUNSET

Profile of BERTHA (ZOOMING) across smooth seas away from
Mobile Bay into open sea. Sunset glows on the horizon . The
sea (GLITTERS) from the sun's reflection on the water. The
sound of powerful engines (ROARING) to life resounds across
the water. Salt water spray (FLIES) into the air as the ship
cuts through the sea.

INT. BERTHA - SUNSET

JAKE stands level once again. He zips his fly and turns
toward the exit door looking back and smiling as he leaves
the bathroom.

BEN is holding JENNY upside down. JENNY is attempting to
push her body up. BEN pulls her up slowly. She stands on her
feet with hands pushing her hair back. BEN stands up to help
her. He wipes his wet shirt with both hands. JENNY is
adjusting her blouse and pants.

                    BEN
          Here, let me help you.

                    JENIFER
          No thanks. I'm fine now. You saved
          me from going overboard. I am
          grateful.

                    BEN
          Are you sure you are OK?

                    JENIFER
          Oh yes. Nothing like being upside
          down on a speeding boat with your
          head between someone's thighs.

                    BEN
          Here, you sit down while I go for
          some drinks. I think we both need
          one after that.

                    JENNY
          Sounds good to me. I think I would
          like one of those "Hillbilly
          Martinis" if you don't mind getting
          me one.

                    BEN
          Stay here. I will be right back.

INT. CAPTAIN' BRIDGE

MATT AND MIKE are looking forward out to sea. MATT notices
KATE holding onto the railing on the forward end of the bow.

                    MATT
          What a woman. She stood there the
          whole time we were coming out of
          the water.

MIKE looks down to the deck.

                                            (CONTINUED)

                         MIKE
          Keep your eye on the ball, boy.
          What is your speed?

                         MATT
          65 Knots. I will slow her to 45 .
          Let the passengers relax a little.

                         MIKE
          Your course heading?

                         MATT
          South, Southeast. Key West. I think
          I will go down on deck. Can you
          hold her steady for a while?

                         MIKE
          I got her. I think I know where you
          are goin'.

MATT gives MIKE the helm and turns to leave the bridge. He
looks back at MIKE.

                         MATT
          I bet you do.

EXT. BERTHA, ON DECK

MATT walks toward KATE . She is standing on the deck looking
out to sea.

                         MATT
          Hello.

KATE turns around and sees MATT approaching.

                         KATE
          Captain,hello. I think some of your
          passengers will be cleaning up
          about right now. Don't you think.

                         MATT
          Maybe. Didn't seem to bother you
          much from where I was sitting.

KATE looks up at the bridge window. She smiles.

                         KATE
          No. Actually I am having a great
          time so far. I hope I can convince
          my parents to do the same. I would
          bet mom is putting blue marks on my
          dad right now.

                         MATT
          I will personally apologize for any
          scare they might have had. Bertha
          likes to move pretty fast and
          deliver a nice ride as quickly as
          possible. Tell you what. I will
          take your dad for a tour of the
          engine room . Do you think he would
          like that?

                         KATE
          I think he would love that.

                         MATT
          Good. Consider it done. Can you
          introduce your parents to me this
          evening sometime?

                         KATE
          Sure. We will be down for dinner
          later and I will look for you.

                         MATT
          Great. See you then.

MATT turns slowly away still looking back at KATE. He bumps
into a very large man dressed in overalls and wearing a long
beard. MATT is stopped by the sudden jolt. He looks up at
the man .

                         MATT (cont'd)
          Sorry sir. Excuse me.

MATT moves away from the gentlemen toward the bridge steps.
KATE is smiling (BROADLY).

INT. BERTHA - EVENING

Passengers are dining in the (GREAT HALL) , a combination
dining and dancing area. A buffet is crowded with people.
BEN is standing in line, JENNY ahead of him. The SPARKS
family is sitting at a long picnic style table. BEN leans
forward toward JENNY.

                         BEN
          Hey there. Are you feeling better
          now?

JENNY turns to look at BEN. Her eyes are glazed. BEN sees
that she has had too much to drink.

                         JENNY
          Are you kidding? I feel great. Come
          on, let's eat some of this stuff.
          Do you know anything about country
          cooking?

                         BEN
          Yea. Sure. Here, let me hold your
          plate and you check out the
          bar.Tell me what you like.

JENNY is looking at the bar (CLOSELY)

                         JENNY
          Well, UH OH.

                         BEN
          What is it?

JENNY throws up all over the buffet. BEN looks on. She gags
repeatedly . Her knees weaken and she begins to drop. BEN
catches her and asks for a wet cloth. He wipes her face and
carries her out to the hallway, holding her against the
wall. She revives. He (STROKES) her cheek.

                         BEN (cont'd)
          Let me take you to your cabin.
          Where is your key?

                         JENNY
          I am so embarrassed.

                         BEN
          You have to sip the "Hillbilly
          Martinis", not drink them down.
          Don't worry, you will feel better
          in the morning.

BEN helps her into the elevator. The door closes.

In the dining room JAKE is eating mounds of food. His mouth
is full.

                         JAKE
          Honey, I am in hog heaven. Those
          ole' boys in the kitchen know what
          they're doin'.

                         NADINE
          That's right baby, I bet you
          they're from Kentucky. I ain't
          never seen so much chicken and
          gravy. Did you try the mashed sweet
          taters?

                    JAKE
          Oh yea. Do you like the way they
          fixed the cornbread and beans? Pass
          me them onions over here JJ. Kids
          we gotta go after that blackberry
          cobbler directly.

JJ farts. JAKE never looks up.

                    JAKE (cont'd)
          That's my boy.

JENELLA moves away (QUICKLY) from JJ. NADINE stares at JJ.

                    NADINE
          Son, I tried to learn you, but you
          just won't teach. This ain't no
          barn. Just cause your daddy ain't
          got a lick of sense don't mean you
          have to act like him.

                    JJ
          Daddy, I can't eat no more. I
          already got a belly full. Can we
          take some cobbler back to the room?

                    JAKE
          Sure boy, you and your sister go up
          there and retrieve a box or
          somethin'. Load her up. We can
          snack on it tonight.

JJ rises from the table with JENELLA. They head for the
buffet and pass by MATT standing at the buffet. MATT is
talking with the BEAUREGARDS.

                    MATT
          Hi there. You must be Mr. and Mrs.
          Beauregard. How are you tonight?

MADDIE looks past MATT toward the buffet. She raises her
hands.

                    MADDIE
          Oh dear lord, the woman vomited all
          over the food. John, take me away
          from here. This is just too much.

                    JOHN
          Calm yourself MADDIE. Let's go
          outside while things are cleaned
          up. Would you excuse us captain?

                                        (CONTINUED)

                         MATT
              Of course. We will have things back
              in order shortly. I will make sure
              you receive the best pickins' on
              the buffet. Please accept my
              apologies.

MADDIE looks at MATT and walks away with JOHN. MATT turns to
KATE.

                         MATT (cont'd)
              Hey, it happens. I hope this won't
              ruin the trip for your mother.

                         KATE
              She'll get over it. A little
              theatrics, nothing serious.

                         MATT
              Good. Would you like to join me for
              dinner?

                         KATE
              I'm starving. Let's do it.

EXT. BERTHA DECK - NIGHT

BEN strolls around the deck and looks at the stars. He sees
a shadow to his left on the starboard side. It looks like a
small person.

                         BEN
              Hello.

No answer. He moves toward the shadow then stops to look
again. The dimly lit deck area allows the shadow to move
away and disappear.

                         BEN (cont'd)
              I must be losing my mind.

BEN walks further down the starboard side deck and enters a
door leading to the cabin hallway. He walks up to an
elevator with it's door open. Inside stands a chimpanzee
next to the elevator buttons. BEN (JUMPS BACK).His mouth
open for a moment.

                         BEN (cont'd)
                    (to monkey)
              What are you doing here?

The ape points at the elevator panel and reaches out toward
BEN with one palm extended upward. BEN steps into the
elevator . The chimp looks at BEN with finger pointed at the
panel buttons. BEN hesitates then shows the monkey two
fingers. The monkey presses floors 2 and 3. Doors close.

The elevator door opens on 2. BEN exits and turns to look at
the monkey. Doors close. BEN stares at he door for a moment.
Turns and walks away.

The elevator door opens on 3. Monkey scampers out of the
elevator down the hall to the captains bridge. Enters and
shuts the bridge door.

INT.BERTHA. 9 PM

MATT is sitting with KATE finishing dinner. The DJ announces
an invitation for music and dancing to all those in the
dining area.

                    DJ
          Folks, if you would enjoy dancing
          and partying now is the time to
          move over this direction.

People are beginning to migrate toward the dance area and
bar.JAKE AND NADINE hear the announcement.

                    JAKE
          Come on baby, let's party.

                    NADINE
          I'm ready.

                    JJ
          Momma, me and Jenella want to stay
          a while. Alright?

                    NADINE
          You two can stay for a little
          while.

MATT and KATE leave the dining table.

                    KATE
          I should take mom and dad some
          food.

                    MATT
          Good idea. Make sure you take some
          dessert. I need to get back to the
          bridge. I'll have some drinks sent
          up in a few minutes.

                              KATE
                    Thanks. I enjoyed tonight.

                              MATT
                    Oh. Please tell your dad I would be
                    happy to take him down for a short
                    tour below deck. Do you think he
                    would be able to do that tonight?

                              KATE
                    I am sure he would. I will have him
                    get in touch with you in a little
                    while.

MATT and KATE leave the hall together as the dance hall
crowd grows larger. The DJ cranks up the sound and plays a
mix of country, rock and contemporary music.The bar is
pumping out drinks by the dozen. "Hillbilly Martinis" are
flowing .

                              DJ
                    Ok everybody, change partners.

He plays, DON'T CHA, by the PUSSY CAT DOLLS. Some of the
female partners dance seductively causing other wives and
girlfriends of the men to react (AGGRESSIVELY). Intentional
bumping and shoving starts and gets out of control. The DJ
sees the shoving and stops the music.

                              DJ (cont'd)
                    Ladies, Ladies, please. Let's all
                    get along here.

The pushing and shoving escalates to fighting among a few of
the women. (CHAOS).

INT. BRIDGE - LATER

MATT is at the wheel. FRANK, the chimpanzee, is perched on
the pad built by MIKE.

                              MATT
                    When did the boys send Frank up?

                              MIKE
                    They called up a few minutes ago
                    and said he was on his way. They
                    wore him out in the engine room
                    handing them tools. I think he is
                    glad to be up here.

                                                          (CONTINUED)

                    MATT
          He knows this boat like the back of
          his hand.

                    MIKE
          He should after three years living
          on Bertha.

                    MATT
          Mike, why don't you get some relief
          and go eat. You need to unwind.
          Tell Dale to relieve you . I am
          going to take Mr. Beauregard down
          below.

MIKE leaves the bridge.

BEAUREGARD CABIN. NIGHT

MADDIE and JOHN are eating. KATE stands at the porthole
window looking out.

                    KATE
          Hey dad, the captain wants to take
          you below deck for a tour. Wanna
          go?

                    JOHN
          Sure. When?

                    KATE
          Now if you want to.

JOHN looks at MADDIE

                    JOHN
          I shouldn't be long. You girls can
          do without me for a while anyway.

JOHN leaves the cabin.

INT. BRIDGE ENTRY DOOR. 5 MINUTES LATER

MATT is checking monitors.

                    MATT
          Frank, get up here and hold the
          wheel steady.

FRANK jumps onto the wheel seat and holds tight to the
wheel. JOHN knocks on the bridge entry door while looking
through the small round window in the door. He sees FRANK
sitting at the wheel.

                    JOHN
               (eyes bulging)
          Oh Lord.

MATT reaches for the door and opens it.

                    MATT
          Hey, how are you? Nice to see you.
          Is something wrong?

MATT turns quickly toward FRANK.

                    MATT (cont'd)
          Oh. Don't worry . We are in good
          hands. Frank here is just holding
          her steady while I check something
          out. Come in, please.

JOHN steps into the bridge cabin. He looks around. MATT has
the second officer take over.

                    MATT (cont'd)
          Dale and Frank will keep it
          straight while we are gone. See you
          boys later.

JOHN and MATT leave the bridge and enter the elevator.

BERTHA'S HULL. NIGHT

The elevator door opens. JOHN and MATT walk out into the
large open area below deck. A series of copper pipes and
holding tanks (LOOM) in front of them. JOHN sees a small
manufacturing facility. He notices steam emanating from one
area. The huge holding tanks extend forward toward the bow.
Beyond is a very large containment tank . To his left is a
doorway. Over it is a sign (engine room).

                    JOHN
          What is all this?

                    MATT
          This is our fuel processing plant.

                    JOHN
          A ship with a fuel processing
          plant?

                    MATT
          Yes sir. We spent about three years
          building it. Bertha is a little
          different than most sea going
          vessels. She has her own refinery.

                    JOHN
          Really?

                    MATT
          She is probably the only ship in
          the world with an ethanol
          processing plant built in the hull.

                    JOHN
          What are you processing with?

                    MATT
          Corn.

JOHN stands quietly looking around.

                    MATT (cont'd)
          Over there is about 65,000 gallons
          of fully processed ethanol from
          corn.

MATT points at the series of holding tanks.

                    MATT (cont'd)
          In the front area you can see the
          corn fuel stock holding area with
          conveyor. It moves the corn into
          the plant. We bleed off some of the
          product for "Hillbilly Martinis".

                    JOHN
               (laughing)
          So, you are moonshining too?

                    MATT
          For personal use only sir , or for
          anyone interested in the taste.

                    JOHN
          Son, I am impressed.

                    MATT
          I had a whole lot of help. MIKE has
          been there with me all the time.My
          dad left me his machine shop and
          that has helped a lot too. We
          managed pretty well.

(CONTINUED)

MATT leads JOHN to the engine room door.

                    MATT (cont'd)
          Sir, you might want to use ear
          protection when we go in.

                    JOHN
          No. that's alright.I'll be fine.

The door opens and they enter. The noise is deafening. MATT
points to the four turbine engines lined up across the room.
He waves at the engine crew. (Thumbs up). JOHN steps around
carefully looking at the engine components. They turn and
leave shutting the door behind them.

                    JOHN (cont'd)
          I'm very impressed young man. Those
          turbine engines provide tons of
          torque. Do you realize what you
          have done here.

                    MATT
          Yes sir. We have a fast boat with a
          range limited only by the fuel
          stock supply. It is cost efficient.

They enter the elevator and stop at the second floor. JOHN
exits the elevator . He turns back and looks at MATT.

                    JOHN
          Matt, I was in the oil business for
          a long time and got rich. You have
          conquered a new world, but some
          people might not like you for it.
          Who else knows about this?

                    MATT
          We built this boat up on Black
          Bayou Inlet. Nobody lives around
          there much. Just me Mike know the
          details. The engine crew is quiet
          about it.

                    JOHN
          Why did you show me all this?

                    MATT
          I could tell you were a man of
          integrity and Kate is a fine woman.
          She could only have been raised by
          good folks. Besides, I promised her
          I would show you around.

                         JOHN
          Thank you. I will talk to you
          later.

                         MATT
          See you later.

Elevator door closes.

INT. BERTHA, DANCE HALL . 11.00 PM

Slow dancing . JAKE holds NADINE and swings her back and
forth.

                         NADINE
          Jake, you are a true romantic man.

                         JAKE
          Thank you darlin.

                         NADINE
          I think we need to go now.

                         JAKE
          Why?

                         NADINE
          You know.

                         JAKE
          Oh yeah. Wait a minute. Where are
          we...

                         NADINE
          There is plenty of hidin' places on
          this big ole' boat.

                         JAKE
          Let's go.

INT. BRIDGE. LATER

MATT, MIKE and FRANK sit on the bridge. MATT checks the
navigational course heading and calculates wind and currents
with the smooth sea ahead of them. He sets BERTHA'S cruising
speed at 65 knots. He sits back.

                         MATT
          Mike, you can rest your eyes a
          while on that cot over there. I
          will keep an eye on the wheel.
          Frank, get up here and go to sleep.

Mike moves off his seat toward the soft cot against the
wall. He fluffs the pillow and lies down.

                    MIKE
          When did you sleep last?

                    MATT
          I don't remember, but I'm fine. I
          will wake you in a few hours. We
          should arrive at Key West early
          morning about 6 am.

                    MIKE
          Goodnight friend.

EXT. BERTHA. AFT. DECK- 5:50 AM

JAKE is holding a cup of coffee as he walks to the rear
deck. Other men are sitting on the swiveling fishing chairs
on BERTHA'S aft deck. It is very early morning. The sun is
just beginning to lighten the sky. BERTHA is moving fast
across a smooth sea.

MATT is sleeping at the wheel as MIKE and FRANK snooze
nearby. BERTHA is nearing the Florida coastline with Tank
island and Wisteria island within sight. The sun rays of
morning are beginning to filter through the bridge forward
windshield causing MATT to blink momentarily. BERTHA is
racing across the sea at 65 knots and closing on Key
West.The cruise control on. MATT blinks again . His eyes
opening. BERTHA enters the idling zone between the two
islands leading into the Key West port. MATT wakes and sees
Key West directly in front. He reaches for the wheel and
turns hard to star board. BERTHA is 1/3 mile from the docks
and closing fast.The turning momentum wakes MIKE and FRANK.
Both jump up and see the harbor. FRANK (SCREAMS AND
CHATTERS). MIKE holds onto the bridge console. MATT is
straining to hold BERTHA in the hard turn. He tries to reach
the throttle handle, but cannot.

BERTHA's profile looks like a huge speedboat creating a huge
wake. She misses several yachts moored in the harbor as she
turns to miss the pier. MATT reaches the throttle and pulls
back hard. BERTHA turns away from the pier in an arching
motion passing nearby boats. The wake (ROCKS) the harbor
waters. Boats bobbing like corks. BERTHA sits down and slows
to a stop. Beside her is a small sailing boat rocking
(FURIOUSLY).

On the rear deck coffee cups are (flying). JAKE and his
companions grip the chair hand rests. Eyes (FROZEN). Mouths
open.

BERTHA IS (STILL). MATT and MIKE are (STARING)silently
through the windshield.

EXT.BERTHA. DECK

JAKE and the boys get off the chairs and walk to the forward
area. They stand next to the railing looking down at the
small sailing boat. Two men emerge from the boat cabin. Both
are dressed only in Speedos. Each are dark tanned.The men
are shaking their fists at JAKE.

                    JAKE
          Howdy boys.

                    MAN NUMBER ONE
          What the hell are you doing, trying
          to kill us.

                    JAKE
          Y'all look fine to me, except for
          those sissy outfits.

                    MAN NUMBER TWO
          You bitch. This is a peaceful haven
          for us. You are barbaric. Where is
          your captain.?

                    JAKE
          Listen little man or whatever you
          are,you can tell your girlfriend to
          fire up that bathtub and leave now,
          or we will launch your butts right
          out of it now.

                    MAN NUMBER ONE
          How dare you. We will be reporting
          this to the authorities.

                    JAKE
          Good. Tell them you were visited by
          aliens if you want to. Now, get
          goin'.

JAKE turns away looking at his buddies as the small craft's
engine starts and the boat moves away quickly.

                    JAKE (cont'd)
          Reckon this here is Key West boys.

BRIDGE

MIKE looks over at MATT sitting in his chair. MATT is
silent and staring straight ahead.. FRANK has his hands over
his ears as MIKE reaches for the intercom handset.

                    MIKE
               (over intercom)
          Good morning everyone. Welcome to
          Key West. Breakfast will be served
          shortly.

BEAUREGARD CABIN

MATT is clutching JOHN as KATE stands looking out the
window.

                    KATE
          We made a real impression on the
          natives didn't we dad?

                    MADDIE
          That is not funny. John that is it.
          We are leaving here as soon as we
          dock.

JENNY'S CABIN

She is (SNORING).

SPARK'S CABIN

NADINE is looking under the bed and in the closet.

                    JJ
          Where is daddy, momma?

                    JENELLA
          Have we lost him?

                    NADINE
          He's around here somewhere, don't
          worry.

NADINE leaves the cabin (RUNNING).

                    NADINE (cont'd)
          Jake Sparks, if you've been killed
          I will never forgive you!

EXT. KEY WEST. DAY

A shore patrol boat pulls up to BERTHA. Officer holds a
bullhorn. MATT is standing outside the bridge . He sees the
boat approach.

                    OFFICER
                 (on bullhorn)
          Cool landing. Awesome in fact. But
          captain, you will have to follow me
          in. Exceeding harbor idle limit.
          There could be other citations.

MATT leans over the railing, cups his hands to his mouth and
(shouts)back.

                    MATT
          We need medical personnel on board.
          I have a sick person on the bridge.
          Please hurry.

MATT goes inside the bridge. BERTHA turns to follow the port
authority boat into harbor.MATT grabs the intercom handset.

                    MATT (cont'd)
          This is the captain. The AC will
          detail the Key West activities as
          we dock. Thank you.

                    MIKE
          Let's get this done and try to
          smooth it over with the port
          authority. Got any ideas?

                    MATT
          Yes. we have an emergency. You are
          ill and passed out on the bridge. I
          couldn't revive you. Frank will
          stay with you while I talk to the
          officer on the pier. I requested an
          ambulance. So, get ready.

                    MIKE
          Are you kidding Matt? They won't
          buy that.

                    MATT
          Yes they will. You just lay still.
          You can regain consciousness when
          the medics arrive. Lord willing, we
          can beat this.

(CONTINUED)

                         MIKE
          Alright, if you think it will work.
          When we dock, you need to let the
          passengers think I am just
          exhausted. That way nobody gets
          freaked out.

                         MATT
          Good idea.

BERTHA pulls up to the North Bight pier. She is tied up.
MATT (RUSHES) to meet the shore patrol officer.

                         MATT
          My first officer is down on the
          bridge. I don't know how bad.

The officer looks at MATT.

                         OFFICER
          What happened?

                         MATT
          He just passed out. Could you get
          them to hurry.

                         OFFICER
          They are on the way. Just relax. I
          think you can go now and just
          remember to keep that ship slow in
          our harbor.

                         MATT
          Thanks officer.

 The ambulance arrives. Medics run with stretcher to board
BERTHA. MATT follows.

INT.BERTHA. DAY

JOHN,MADDY AND KATE are eating breakfast in the dining hall.

                         MADDY
          John, use your cell and call in the
          pilot.

                         JOHN
          I do wish you would change your
          mind. We will be in St. Thomas by
          tomorrow and you know how nice it
          is there.

MADDY looks at JOHN.

                    MADDY
          Call him.

                    KATE
          I think I will stay with the
          cruise. Are you guys OK with that?

                    MADDY
          It is up to you dear. I just can't
          take all this excitement.

                    KATE
          I understand. Well, I am going to
          do a little shopping and maybe some
          snorkeling here in Key West.
          Anybody game for that?

                    JOHN
          I think your mother has a greater
          need for rest. You go on and have a
          good time. We will see you before
          we leave.

KATE is leaving the dining area.

                    KATE
          OK. I'll see you guys later.

JENNY'S CABIN

BEN knocks on JENNY'S cabin door. No answer. He knocks twice
more. No answer. BEN turns to walk away.

                    JENNY
          Come on in.

                    BEN
          Are you decent?

                    JENNY
               (moaning)
          Yes...

BEN enters the cabin.JENNY is lying in bed with a cold
washcloth on her head. Eyes bloodshot. Makeup ruined.

                    BEN
          Can I get you anything?

                    JENNY
          Yes. A gun. I'm going to put myself
          out of misery.

                         BEN
          Come on. Let's get you up. I have
          the medicine you need for your
          ailment.Get dressed. I'll be back
          in a minute. Trust me, you will be
          better in no time.

BEN exits the cabin and walks to the elevator. The doors
open and EMTs are pushing a stretcher out. BEN stands to the
side and watches them roll the stretcher toward the bridge.

The EMTs enter the bridge. MATT leads them in. MIKE is lying
on the floor. FRANK is on top of MIKE with his arms wrapped
around MIKE. The EMTs stand looking at the scene.

EXT. DOCKSIDE - DAY

MIKE is rolled down the gangway on the stretcher. He has an
oxygen mask over his face. MATT is standing on the dock as
the stretcher passes by. MIKE looks up and (WINKS) at MATT.

PASSENGERS are leaving the ship and stand watching the EMTs
moving MIKE. BEN and JENNY move down the gangway following.

                         JENNY
          The captain said he would be OK.
          Just exhaustion. What is this drink
          you brought me?

                         BEN
          A little hair of the dog with
          tomato juice and Goody's powders.
          You like it?

                         JENNY
          I feel a little better already.
          Thanks.

EXT. KEY WEST SHOPPING DISTRICT - AFTERNOON

The SPARKS family is shopping for beach wear. Jake looks at
bright colored baggy shorts. NADINE is holding up a bikini.
JJ and JENELLA are walking through the shop.

                         JAKE
          Hey baby, look here.

JAKE holds up the pair of shorts. Yellow with red polka
dots.

                                                    (CONTINUED)

                    NADINE
          Those are you baby. What about this
          bikini?

                    JAKE
          Sizzlin' hot darlin'.

On the street locals are eyeballing the assortment of
country people. The NEWLYWED couple is riding in an electric
mini car. A street vendor approaches them at a stop light.

                    STREET VENDOR
          You folks interested in a good deal
          on sunglasses with MP3s built in?

He holds up a pair.

                    NEWLYWED MAN
          No thanks. We can hear just fine.
          No need for the aids.

                    STREET VENDOR
          NO. NO. NO. These are the latest.
          Sunglasses with a music player. You
          just put them in your ears like
          this.

He demonstrates.

                    NEWLYWED MAN
          How much?

                    STREET VENDOR
          Fifty bucks a pair. Two hundred in
          stores. Want em?

                    NEWLYWED MAN
          Do you like shine?

                    STREET VENDOR
          Moonshine?

                    NEWLYWED MAN
          Yep.

                    STREET VENDOR
          Sure.

                    NEWLYWED MAN
          This here is yours for the glasses.

He holds up a quart jar. It (shimmers) in the sunlight.

                                              (CONTINUED)

                         STREET VENDOR
              Deal.

Exchange is made. Off goes the mini car .Newlywed couple
wearing MP3s.

JAKE AND FAMILY ride along the streets dressed in beach
wear. They are on a four seater bicycle.JAKE is on the front
seat.

KATE is on the beach. She is walking into the water with
snorkel gear.

EXT BERTHA DECKSIDE . LATER

JOHN and MADDIE are sitting in deck chairs.JOHN is talking
on cell phone.

                         JOHN
              No.We did not know that. When will
              it get here? (Pause). You serious?
              When can you get here? (Pause).
              That will be too late. I will get
              back to you. Stay put.

                         MADDIE
              What is it John?

JOHN speed dials KATE. Looks at MADDIE.

                         JOHN
                     (to MADDIE)
              There is a major hurricane off the
              Florida east coast near Miami. It
              was upgraded from tropical. The
              weather advisory is for a watch. It
              will hit the coast in a few short
              hours.

KATE'S cell phone rings. It is buried in her beach bag. She
is snorkeling. JOHN leaves a voice mail.

                         MADDIE
              So. What are we going to do?

                         JOHN
              You stay here. Try Kate again. I
              will see the captain.

JOHN rises up and walks up the stairway to the bridge. He
knocks. MATT opens the door.

                    MATT
          Come in sir.

JOHN steps inside.

                    MATT (cont'd)
          Have you heard about the storm?

                    JOHN
          Yes. What is going on?

                    MATT
          We have monitored the weather and
          it looks like a tropical storm
          turned into a hurricane real quick.

                    JOHN
          How is it tracking?

                    MATT
          Straight this way.

                    JOHN
          What's the ETA?

                    MATT
          Four to six hours. I have tried to
          reach the passengers. The AC gave
          all of them his cell number before
          they went ashore. I hope the locals
          alert them soon so they will get
          back here. We can get out of here
          quick if we need to.Did you get
          hold of Kate?

                    JOHN
          Voice message. She's swimming.

                    MATT
          I have to leave. Would you excuse
          me?

                    JOHN
          Sure. You think we could outrun the
          storm?

MATT is walking out the bridge doorway.

                    MATT
          Bertha can take us out of harm's
          way. These big boats can't do that.
          If this storm is bad, we need to
          get out fast.

INT. KEY WEST LOCAL TELEVISION 3 PM

Public announcement. Weatherman shows track of storm
approaching.

INT. KEY WEST HOSPITAL - DAY

MIKE pulls the IVs out of his arm and gets dressed. He
leaves the hospital unnoticed. Black cloud formations loom .
A cab driver pulls up. MIKE gets in.

                    MIKE
          Take me to the Bight pier, please.

                    CABBY
          Hey buddy, you heard about the
          hurricane headed this way?

                    MIKE
          Yes.Can you drive a little faster?

INT. BERTHA. DECK

JOHN AND MADDIE standing against the port side railing. They
are looking at the cloud formations. Lightning appears in
the distance. The wind is beginning to increase.

                    JOHN
          Captain says we will leave soon and
          outrun this storm. Don't worry.

                    MADDIE
          Call Kate again.

JOHN dials. NO answer. He snaps the phone shut.

EXT. KEY WEST BIGHT - DAY

Four young men carrying heavy steel lines coiled up walk
down a pathway and into the water near BERTHA'S stern.

Dockside, the two men BERTHA just missed entering the
harbor, stand watching the four young men enter the water
and disappear. MATT passes by them .

                    MAN ON DOCK
          Hey captain, you better get
          that double wide trailer out of
          here. You know how they attract
          tornadoes.

                    MATT
          You gentlemen have a nice day here
          in Key West.

MIKE gets out of a cab at the pier. MATT walks quickly
toward him.

                    MIKE
          Hey buddy. I just heard. Are we
          ready to leave?

                    MATT
          Gotta round up the passengers. The
          word's out, but I can't predict
          when they will all get back.

                    MIKE
          Check the AC. He might have gotten
          calls from some of the passengers.

                    MATT
          Already did. Most of them are on
          the way back now.

                    MIKE
          It's deteriorating fast. Let's get
          to the bridge and monitor the
          storm.

MIKE and MATT turn toward BERTHA.

KEY WEST BEACH - DAY

BEN and JENNY stand in ankle deep water looking at the cloud
formations.

                    BEN
          I guess we should be getting back.

                    JENNY
          You have really taken good care of
          me today. Why are you being so
          nice?I'm not used to that.

                    BEN
          You should be used to it.

JENNY reaches for BEN and puts her arms around him.

                    JENNY
          What are you doing to me?

                                            (CONTINUED)

                              BEN
                    I was about to ask you the same
                    question.

Lightning (STRIKES) in the distance.

                              BEN (cont'd)
                    We gotta go now.

They leave the beach.

SPARKS FAMILY

JAKE is peddling as fast as he can as JJ,JENELLA and NADINE
peddle (furiously) behind him on the four person bike.

EXT. BERTHA DOCKSIDE

Passengers arrive at the pier for boarding. The AC stands on
the gangway with a clipboard. He is checking off each
arrival. Lightning and winds gusting.(BOOMING) sounds in the
distance. The water is choppy in the harbor.

KATE ON BEACH.

KATE walks quickly out of the sea and gets into her mini
car.

DOCKSIDE

MIKE looks at the AC

                              MIKE
                    Is everyone accounted for now?

                              AC
                    Except for the Sparks family. I
                    believe that is all.

                              MIKE
                    Keep a sharp eye. I gotta get up to
                    the bridge.

The SPARKS family is racing onto the pier, pedaling the
bicycle as fast as it will go. JAKE turns hard to his left
avoiding the edge of the pier and the bicycle slides out
from under them. The AC comes to their aid and helps NADINE
up. JAKE gathers the children and all climb the gangway
slowly.

The sky turns dark. Winds whipping around the pier. The Port
Authority Alarm sounds. KATE is flying through the streets
of Key West.

INT. BERTHA - LATE AFTERNOON

MATT sits at the wheel and uploads the latest radar
forecasting on the storm. MIKE is on the radio with the
engine room. MATT leaves the bridge and hurries down the
outside steps, sliding down the railing onto the deck. He
grabs his nextel while walking to the crewman casting off
the ropes.

                    MATT
          Mike, are we ready to move out?

                    MIKE
          Yes sir, captain. Give the word.

                    MATT
          Well, I just saw three waterspouts
          behind us. Back home we call them
          tornadoes. Get going now.

                    MIKE
          Roger.

BERTHA moves forward. The steel lines underneath her hull
are attached to the pier and begin to strain and tighten.

MATT sees KATE jumping from her mini car and running toward
him as BERTHA slides along the pier. She (WAVES) her arms as
she reaches the end of the pier. MATT (STARES) at KATE.

BERTHA surges forward and the lines underneath the hull
strain and twist tightly. The pier (EXPLODES) underneath
KATE. She is thrown into the water and debris. MATT dives
into the water and swims toward her. KATE comes to the
surface (GASPING) for air. MATT reaches for her and grabs
one arm. He holds onto her tightly.

MIKE uses his nextel.

                    MIKE (cont'd)
          Matt, come back.

No answer. MIKE repeats. No answer. The deck crewman calls
to MIKE.

                    CREWMAN
          Man overboard. Stop the vessel.

                    MIKE
          Roger.

BERTHA slows and reverses thrust. MIKE radios.

(CONTINUED)

                         MIKE (cont'd)
          Crewman, where is the captain.

                         CREWMAN
          Rescuing a passenger. Over.

A line is thrown out. MATT holds KATE and reaches for the
line. They are pulled aboard BERTHA.

                         CREWMAN (cont'd)
          They are safe on board. We are
          clear to depart.

The engines rev and BERTHA surges forward moving fast across
the harbor. MIKE throttles up. BERTHA planes out. BERTHA
moves past Wisteria and Tank islands.

MATT helps KATE to her feet. Both are soaking wet. Towels
are thrown around them. They move inside. MATT borrows the
crewman's radio.

                         MATT
          Mike. We are clear. Push her faster
          South Southeast.Tell the
          Beauregards Kate is with me and is
          OK.

                         MIKE
          Welcome aboard captain. Over.

INT. BERTHA - LATE AFTERNOON . OUT TO SEA

BERTHA speeds out to sea. The sky is clear. To the north
behind them ominous cloud formations loom across the
horizon. MATT is at the helm. MIKE beside him.

                         MATT
          That was a close one. Somebody back
          there decided to tie us up to the
          pier.

                         MIKE
          It appears that way. Oh. we don't
          have GPS. The computer is blinked
          out right now. I will work on it.

                         MATT
          I will set the course with the
          chart. We should be fine.

KATE knocks on the bridge door. MIKE reaches to open it.

                    MIKE
          There is the late comer. You look
          well. Are you?

                    KATE
               (smiling)
          Yes. Thanks to you guys.

,She walks over and puts her hand on MATT'S shoulder.

                    KATE (cont'd)
          Thanks.

She kisses MATT.

                    MATT
          I would do it everyday if I thought
          this would happen.

FRANK reaches for KATE. She picks him up. He hugs her
tightly.

                    KATE
          Mom and dad are still aboard. I
          guess the positive is the storm
          changed mom's mind about leaving
          the cruise.

                    MATT
          That's a good thing isn't it?

KATE smiles.

                    KATE
          Are we headed to ST. Thomas?

                    MATT
          Yes. Should be there in a few
          hours. I am going to slow her down.
          The sun is still high enough for
          the passengers to enjoy the rest of
          the day . Seas are calm. I think it
          is time for everybody to have some
          fun.

                    KATE
          Can you guys come to dinner with
          me? You need some downtime too.

                    MIKE
          I think we can do that. I will get
          some people up here to take the
          watch.

                    KATE
          Great. See you guys later.

KATE leaves the bridge. MATT slows BERTHA to 30 knots.

INT. GREAT HALL 6 PM

The hall is full of people eating and drinking. BEN AND
JENNY are eating together a at large round table. The
BEAUREGARDS are looking for a table and see empty seats at
BEN and JENNY's table.

                    KATE
          Would you mind if we join you?

                    JENNY
          Not at all. Please.

The BEAUREGARDS are seated.

MIKE and MATT enter the dining hall. KATE notices. She
stands to toast MATT. The room (ERUPTS)with applause for the
captain. MATT bows his head then looks up.

                    MATT
          Folks , there is no need for this.
          We thought it would be better to
          escape the storm than to stay in
          town and enjoy it.

(LAUGHTER) breaks out in the hall. KATE signals for MATT AND
MIKE to join them.

                    MATT (cont'd)
          Everybody just keep eating. We are
          going to make this a good cruise, I
          promise.

KITCHEN (GALLEY)

Activity in the kitchen (galley). A cook dressed in a white
chef's apron steps through a rear hatchway. He steps down to
a fantail deck and reaches for a large net. He throws it out
and calls up to the bridge.

                    COOK
          Hey up there. Cut the speed to 5
          knots. It is fishin' time. Catch of
          the day. Over.

BERTHA slows to a crawl. The cook dumps five gallon buckets
of chicken scraps as the net extends out to sea. Schools of
fish appear . Another cook comes out of the hatchway.

                    COOK ASSISTANT
          Are you ready?

                    COOK
          Yes . Hand it to me.

The assistant hands a stick of marine dynamite to the cook.
He lights it and throws it into the water behind the boat.A
deep,loud (BOOM) follows with water jetting upward.The
waiting net gathers the fish floating on top of the sea. A
winch pulls the net closer to the fantail deck. Both cooks
haul the fish in. Others reach to sort the catch and take it
into the kitchen for preparation.

The net is rolled up. The cooks disappear into the kitchen.
Inside fresh catch is cleaned and cooking .

                    COOK
                 (ON RADIO)
          Catch is done. Thanks. Over.

BERTHA'S speed increases. Sharks follow the boat.

DINING HALL - SUNSET

Around the dining table, MADDIE converses with JENNY.

                    MADDIE
          Are you and Ben married?

                    JENNY
          Oh no, we just met.

                    MADDIE
          Really, when was that?

                    JENNY
          We met in a taxi and then I found
          myself upside down between his
          legs. Since then, we have become
          good friends.

Everyone at the table is speechless. BEN (squirms in his
chair). MATT looks at KATE. JOHN breaks the silence.

                    JOHN
          Well, how nice. Why don't we order
          more drinks. Would anyone like a
          Hillbilly martini?

                         MADDIE
               Get me a double please.

                         KATE
               I'll take some wine .

                         MATT
               OK. Let me go to the bar. Kate
               would you like to walk with me?

                         KATE
               Sure. Hey Ben, can we get you and
               Jenny something?

                         BEN
               Jenny , I think I'll have a martini
               too. Do you want one?

                         JENNY
               No thanks. It could end up on the
               salad bar like the last one.

MADDIE is staring straight at JENNY. (eyes wide).

                         KATE
               Alright then. Would you like
               something else.

                         JENNY
               Some water please.

Kate (nods). She and MATT walk away.

                         (INTERCOM)
               Please join us for fireworks after
               sundown. You can find good seats on
               the upper deck around the pool or
               anywhere deck side. Night fishing
               will begin afterwards on the rear
               deck. Thank you.

EXT. BERTHA - LATER

The dance hall music filters outside where many passengers
are observing fireworks. The top deck is crowded with young
people. The sky is black and the vault of the universe is
full of bright stars. Smoke drifts away from BERTHA as a
cascade of fireworks explodes upward.

MATT and KATE join others on the star board side of the
boat. KATE finds her mother as JOHN and MATT stand facing
each other with drinks in hand.

                                                        (CONTINUED)

                         JOHN
               Beautiful evening captain.

                         MATT
               Yes sir, it is.

MATT is distracted by someone asking him a question. He
turns to his left. JOHN is leaning against the railing when
the boat moves slightly and he loses his balance. He falls
backward into the sea.

MATT turns back to speak to JOHN and finds him missing. KATE
approaches MATT.

                         KATE
               Matt, have you seen dad? Mom needs
               to ask him something.

                         MATT
               He was just here. I guess he got
               bored and walked away.

Fishermen on the rear deck sitting in swivel chairs are
baiting lines and casting out. A fishing rod bends in half
as the fisherman pulls and reels.

                         FISHERMAN
               Boys, I got a big one this time!

He hauls and pulls as onlookers gather around.

                         FISHERMAN (cont'd)
               Throw that spotlight on the water,
               quick.

A large flood of light hits the churning sea below BERTHA's
stern. A figure of a man appears to be thrashing around. He
is hooked from the lower crotch to his belt missing his
flesh. The bait fish is (flopping) on the hook at his
crotch. Someone in the crowd recognizes the face.

                         PASSENGER I
               That is Mr. Beauregard!

Crewmen throw a line with a float attached. Several men
reach over the side. JOHN is hauled in on the fishing line
and someone loops the rope around his body. He is hauled up
the side of the boat. Floodlights expose the horror on his
face. His pants waistline is pulled up around his chest and
one shoe is missing. He clutches the martini glass in one
hand.

MADDIE and KATE look at the spectacle.

                         MADDIE
              Oh dear God, please get him aboard.
              John.. Kate help your daddy. Please
              someone bring him to me...

JOHN is safely brought aboard soaking wet.His clothing
tattered. MADDIE surges through the crowd to his side.

                         MADDIE (cont'd)
              Oh, darling . Are you OK. Please
              speak to me John Beauregard.

JOHN looks up at MADDIE.

                         JOHN
              I am quite alright dear. Just get
              someone to extract this fish from
              my groin.

MATT and KATE lead him toward the nearest entry way to the
cabins.

                         MATT
              OK everybody. It's over. Please
              continue fishing. Thanks for your
              help.

INT. BERTHA'S BRIDGE - NIGHT

FRANK is sitting on his perch pad stand looking out the
window. MATT is trying to re boot the computer programming.
MIKE is charting the course to St. Thomas manually.

KATE comes onto the bridge and closes the door.

                         KATE
              Dad is fine. Mom is babying him.
              They went back down to have a
              drink.

                         MATT
              Do you want to take the wheel for a
              few minutes?

                         KATE
              Are you sure?

                         MATT
              Get up here and try it.

KATE sits at the wheel.

                                              (CONTINUED)

                         MATT (cont'd)
          Just hold her steady. You're doing
          just fine. Mike, do you want to go
          down for a rest?

                         MIKE
          Yes. I think I will. You two can
          handle this for now. Thanks.

MIKE leaves. MATT sits behind a computer screen. FRANK is
watching KATE.

                         MIKE (cont'd)
          So, what are you going to do after
          graduate school?

                         KATE
          I'm not sure. Dad wants me to take
          over some of his business, but
          marine biology puts me close to the
          sea where I belong. How about you?
          Think you will like the cruise
          business?

                         MATT
          A lot depends on how this cruise
          balances out after we get back. I
          can always sell BERTHA if I have
          to.

                         KATE
          What about family?

                         MATT
          It is just me. Mike is retired and
          widowed. Frank over there is my
          only child.(laughs). I have a
          sister in Oklahoma.

FRANK looks at MATT and chatters then moves over to KATE'S
side. He reaches for her shorts leg and tugs. She reaches
down and pulls him up onto the seat with her.

                         MATT (cont'd)
          Do you plan on settling down , get
          married, have children, the house
          and white picket fence thing?

                         KATE
          I don't see the picket fence, but I
          do see the man.

She glances over at MATT and back to the wheel. MATT raises his eyes from the computer screen and turns them toward her.FRANK (chatters loudly).

DANCE HALL 11:00 PM

JAKE is sweating and dancing to a rock song with NADINE. JOHN and MADDIE are drinking at a table nearby. The bartender is moving quickly to fill drink orders. The dance floor is full. An old couple dance in the center of the dance floor. People watch them moving around. The song ends.

                    DISC JOCKEY
          Folks , this has been on heck of an
          evening. We are going to take a
          break now. Be back in a few
          minutes.

A waitress walks up to the BEAUREGARD'S table and hands an 8x10 glossy photo of JOHN to MADDIE.

                    WAITRESS
          Someone here made this for you. I
          hope you like it.

The waitress leaves. MADDIE looks at the photo of JOHN. It shows him suspended from the rescue line with fish hook in his pants. She hands it to JOHN.

                    MADDIE
          That's one for the family album.

                    JOHN
          A pretty good likeness, wouldn't
          you say?

INT.BERTHA BRIDGE - MIDNIGHT

MATT is at the wheel. KATE is holding FRANK. MATT increases speed to 60 knots. BERTHA (GLIDES) across open seas leaving a long wake spray.

                    MATT
          I think it is time to get some
          sleep. I am going to let the second
          officer take the watch. FRANK, you
          have had enough attention from KATE
          for one night. It is my turn.

                         KATE
              Leave him alone. He is just a big
              baby. Isn't that right boy?

FRANK holds KATE tighter. She sets him down on his pad. She
and MATT leave the bridge. The night watch takes over.

EXT. BERTHA. SUNRISE. 6 AM

A cook stands on the deck smoking a cigarette. The morning
sunrise lifts the darkness as BERTHA speeds across blue
waters. The cook notices a coastline in the distance. He
puffs on the cigarette, throws it into the sea and goes
inside.

CUT TO BRIDGE

On the bridge, the SECOND OFFICER and mate look to star
board and see the coastline lengthening.

                         SECOND OFFICER
                    (to mate)
              Go raise the captain. We may have a
              problem.

He looks at the chart and runs his index finger across the
map.

                         SECOND OFFICER (cont'd)
              Tell him it is very important. Go.

The mate moves quickly off the bridge. The SECOND OFFICER
looks to the coastline. He studies his chart and maps.

CUT TO

JAKE moves down the hallway holding a cup of coffee. He
exits the rear deck exit door and joins other men sitting on
the swiveling fishing chairs. The wind blows around BERTHA's
superstructure and (WHISTLES) by the men sitting on the
chairs.

CUT TO

MATT enters the bridge. The SECOND officer looks up from the
chart.

                         SECOND OFFICER (cont'd)
              Good morning sir. We may have a
              problem with navigation. Could you
              take a look?

MATT bends down and studies the chart as he glances out to
see the coastline.

                    MATT
          We should not be seeing coastline.
          Little Ragged Island should be
          miles south of us. That coastline
          is too long. (pause) . All stop.

The crew slows BERTHA and sets her down into the sea. MATT
uses binoculars and is looking closely at the coastline. The
SECOND OFFICER peers at the coastline through binoculars.

                    MATT (cont'd)
          Someone wake Mike. Get him up here
          now.

A crewman leaves the bridge. MATT is looking through the
binoculars and sees a small high speed boat approaching .

                    MATT (cont'd)
          We have company boys.

                                                      REAR DECK

JAKE is facing another man on the swivel chairs.

                    JAKE
          Reckon why we stopped so fast?

                    OTHER MAN
          Don't rightly know.

Another man sitting on the star board side chair sees the
speed boat approaching quickly. He points toward the boat.

                    PASSENGER II
          Look there boys, we got somebody
          comin' in on us fast.

All heads turn.

                                                        BRIDGE

MATT AND MIKE leave the bridge and climb down the star board
side steps to the deck. The speeding boat slows and turns
toward them. It is a 30 foot V hull with four men dressed in
black outfits. One is wearing a hat. Guns are held by 3 of
the men. The craft eases up to BERTHA and idles. The driver
reaches for a bullhorn. He looks at MATT standing on the
railing.

                                                  (CONTINUED)

                         DRIVER
                        (Spanish)
                 Identify yourself. We are coming
                 aboard now.

MATT looks at MIKE.

                         MATT
                 What the hell did he say?

                         MIKE
                 I don't know, but that flag he is
                 flying is strange looking. Where
                 the hell are we?

                         MATT
                 I am not sure, but I won't let
                 terrorists board my ship.

MATT cups his hands to his mouth and looks toward the boat
driver.

                         MATT (cont'd)
                 You better identify yourself first.
                 Comprende?

The driver turns to one of his men and points at the Alabama
State flag flying on top of BERTHA.

                         DRIVER
                        (Spanish)
                 That flag is one of pirates. The
                 red cross on white flag.Fire a
                 round over her bow.

The man raises his machine gun and fires over BERTHA.
(bam,bam,bam).

The star board side port hole windows on BERTHA swing open
one at a time. Shotguns and pistols appear aimed at the
speed boat crewmen. The (clicking) sound of guns being
cocked . The only sound is water (lapping) against the sides
of the two boats.

A cook steps out on the deck with a stick of dynamite. He is
smoking a cigar. He stands still.

MATT and MIKE stand silent for a few seconds. MATT looks
down at the driver and leans over with his hands cupped to
his mouth.

                         MATT
             I believe it is time for you boys
             to take a swim. Now!

MIKE shows swimming (gestures) with his arms extended. The
Spanish speaking crew see him.

A shot is fired from one of the port holes. (BOOM)

The four crewmen dive overboard and swim away from the speed
boat. The cook puts the dynamite fuse to the lit end of the
cigar. He throws it in an arching motion into the speed
boat. (BOOM).

Fire erupts and the fuel tanks (EXPLODE). Shotgun and pistol
fire (THUNDERS) across the water. Smoke (Billows) from the
small boat as fire (LEAPS) skyward.

One by one, the port hole windows on BERTHA close shut. The
cook puffs on the cigar,his gold teeth (SHINING). He turns
and leaves. MATT and MIKE stand in silence watching the
burning hulk drift away.

                         MATT (cont'd)
             You reckon those fellows can swim
             to shore before the sharks get em'?

                         MIKE
             They will set some records today.

Matt turns to walk toward the bridge steps. MIKE follows.

                                                    AFT DECK

Jake and the boys are holding coffee cups as the burning
boat drifts by them.

                         JAKE
             That'll learn em' to speak American
             next time.

A man sitting next to JAKE sips a cup of coffee.

                         MAN NUMBER TWO
             Yep. We won't get took over by them
             towel heads disguised as pirates.

BRIDGE- MINUTES LATER

MATT eases BERTHA forward and away from the burning boat. He sees the crew (BOBBING) in the sea like corks in BERTHA's wake.

                    MATT
          Did you recognize that flag?

                    MIKE
          No. since we don't know exactly
          where we are, I would say they are
          renegades from a small island
          somewhere out here.

                    MATT
          I think we should bring them aboard
          and find out who they are. We can
          lock them up if need be until we
          reach St. Thomas.

                    MIKE
          You're the captain. It is your
          call.

                    MATT
          Go down and notify the AC we need
          to have a meeting in the hall in a
          few minutes. I need to talk to the
          passengers about all this.

Mike steps away to the bridge door.

                    MATT (cont'd)
          Hey. Send two guys up here with
          guns. We'll turn around and scoop
          those fellows out of the water.

                    MIKE
          Got it.

EXT. BERTHA - DAY

BERTHA moves close to the Spanish crew floating in the water. Crewmen pull the survivors aboard. MATT stands by and looks for the driver of the speed boat. He points to the man with a hat on his head.

                    MATT
          Bring him here.

The water drenched uniformed man is led to MATT. They look at each other. MATT raises his nextel.

                         MATT (cont'd)
                    (to Mike)
               See if you can get Kate to come
               down here. She knows some Spanish.
               Over.

                         MIKE
               Roger.

MATT looks into the eyes of the uniformed man.

                         MATT
               Can you speak English?

                         SPANISH MAN
               A little.

                         MATT
               Who are you?

                         SPANISH MAN
               I am Cuban naval officer. You in my
               waters. You understand?

MATT (stares) at the Cuban.

                                                    BEAUREGARD CABIN

MIKE knocks on the door. KATE opens the door.

                         MIKE
               Kate, can you come with me? Matt
               needs some Spanish interpreted.

                         KATE
               Sure. What's going on out there?

                         MIKE
               You'll see. Ready?

KATE leaves the cabin with MIKE.

                                                              DECK

KATE walks with MIKE approaching MATT from behind.

                         KATE
               What is going on here?

MATT turns to see KATE

                                                    (CONTINUED)

                    MATT
          Can you interpret Spanish for me?

                    KATE
          Yes.

                    MATT
          It appears we have drifted into
          Cuban waters. We are way off
          course. He is a Cuban naval officer
          and we blew his boat out of the
          water.

                    KATE
          OK. OK. Whatever you want me to do.

                    MATT
               (to crewmen)
          Take those three down to crew
          quarters and give them dry clothes.

The men are escorted away by the crewmen.

                    MATT (cont'd)
          Ask him where he lives and the
          distance to his port from here.

KATE interprets.

                    CUBAN CAPTAIN
               (Spanish)
          I need to call base in Puerto
          Gibara. You are four miles from my
          base. I cannot tell my people that
          my boat was sunk by an American
          cruise ship. I would be humiliated
          and court martialed.

KATE interprets.

                    MATT
          Tell him I understand his position.
          Also, tell him we are very sorry
          for destroying his boat. We
          believed he was a terrorist or
          renegade.

KATE interprets.

                    CUBAN CAPTAIN
               (Spanish)
          I thought you were a pirate ship or
          group of misfits. Your flag is one
          of pirates.

KATE interprets.

                    MATT
          Tell him he can go to my cabin and
          clean up. We will take care of him
          and his crew. When he dries out we
          will speak again. I need to speak
          with the passengers and let them
          know what is going on here.

KATE interprets.

CUT TO

FRANK slides down the bridge railing and scampers to MATT'S
side. He reaches out for the Cuban Captain's hand. The Cuban
is escorted by FRANK and a crewman to the hall elevator .

JAKE enters the elevator with the three. The elevator goes
up. FRANK (FARTS). JAKE leans over and pushes the elevator
button several times. FRANK puts his hands over his mouth
and nose. The CUBAN steps back with the crewman.

CAMERA POV from hallway on third floor.

The elevator doors open. JAKE steps out quickly closely
followed by the CUBAN and CREWMAN. FRANK follows . His hands
on his face.

INT. DINING HALL - MORNING

MATT stands in front of the passengers. He holds a
microphone. There is silence in the hall.

                    MATT
          Good morning everybody. I guess you
          know by now that a Cuban vessel
          approached our star board side and
          was destroyed. This happened quite
          by accident as there was a mis
          communication between me and the
          captain of the Cuban boat. The
          captain would like for us to take
          him and his crew to Puerto Gibara a
          few miles from here. We can do
          that, but I want you to know it is
          up to you folks. We can take them
          home or to ST. Thomas and let the
          authorities handle it from there.
          So a vote is in order. We do not
          know at this point how the Cuban
          authorities will view this
          situation, so keep that in mind .

Sound of passengers talking with each other. JAKE stands up
and raises his hand toward MATT.

                    JAKE
          We don't need those boys on this
          boat. Take em' home.

JOHN stands.

                    JOHN
          Captain, this will create an
          international incident either way.
          I suggest we go forward now and
          take a vote.

                    MATT
          OK. All in favor of taking these
          guys to their port in Cuba raise
          your hands.

MADDIE stands quickly.

                    MADDIE
          Captain, wait a minute. If we take
          them to Cuba will we likely be
          paraded on national television and
          get a tour of Puerto Gibara or
          whatever it is called?

                    MATT
          That or put in detention for a
          while.

MADDIE sits down.

                    MATT (cont'd)
          Alright, all in favor raise your
          hands.

All passengers raise their hands. MADDIE hesitates. Everyone
looks at her. She raises her hand. She looks at JOHN.

                    MADDIE
          John, get me a martini. No, make it
          a double.

INT. BRIDGE- FIVE MINUTES LATER

MATT, MIKE, KATE and the CUBAN CAPTAIN stand next to the
radio. The CUBAN holds the handset. MATT looks at KATE.

                                              (CONTINUED)

                    MATT
          Tell me every word he says.

KATE nods.

                    CUBAN CAPTAIN
                (SPANISH)
          This is Captain Alvarez to base.
          Over. (Pause).

                    OTHER END
          Roger, go ahead.

                    CUBAN CAPTAIN
          Our vessel is damaged by fire. We
          abandoned ship. Notify authorities
          we were picked up by an American
          cruise ship. Get instructions right
          away. The Americans are friendly.

                    OTHER END
          Roger. Will report back. Please
          wait.

KATE interprets.

                    MIKE
          Matt, they'll be coming for us now.

                    MATT
          Crank her up. Let's be ready to
          move, just in case.

                    MIKE
          Good idea. I'll do it.

MIKE starts the engines.

The sound of engines warming (DEEP RUMBLE).

BERTHA'S DECK

BEN and JENNY are standing on the bow deck looking at the
coastline.

                    JENNY
          What is going to happen now Ben?

                    BEN
          Oh. we'll probably be political
          prisoners for life.(laughs)

JENNY turns and stares at BEN.

                         BEN (cont'd)
          Listen, I am just joking, but it
          will be interesting. Something
          you'll never forget.

They see airplanes approaching in the distance.

BRIDGE - LATER

The radio crackles. Spanish is spoken. CAPTAIN ALVAREZ holds
the handset.

                         CUBAN CAPTAIN
          Roger. What? Would you repeat
          please. Over.

                         OTHER END
          El Presidente requests the presence
          of the American captain in Havana.
          Escort planes and boats will be
          arriving soon.

                         CUBAN CAPTAIN
          Roger. I will tell the captain.
          Over.

KATE interprets to MATT. The CUBAN turns to look at MATT,
his eyes wide and mouth open.The sound of (WHOOSHING) as
fighter jets pass low over BERTHA. In the distance a large
patrol boat moves toward BERTHA.

                         MATT
          Here comes the welcoming committee.

                         KATE
          I guess we are going to Havana.

                         MATT
          It is over 450 miles back up the
          coast. That will set us back
          another day at least. OK, let's
          move out. We will let them know
          Bertha could have outrun any of
          their boats. That will let them
          know we are the good guys.

MATT takes the helm and intercoms the passengers.

                         MATT (cont'd)
          Attention please. We will be moving
          very fast . Our destination is
          Havana,Cuba. Please be seated
                         (MORE)

                         MATT (cont'd)
          until Bertha levels at speed.
          Thanks.

MATT eases BERTHA around heading toward Havana. He gently
pushes the throttle forward. KATE and FRANK at his side.
BERTHA rises slowly. MATT pushes forward again. BERTHA
surges forward in the clear smooth waters. BERTHA reaches
cruising speed of 70 knots and levels out.

EXT. PROFILE OF BERTHA SPEEDING ACROSS THE SEA. BOATS
CHASING HER. JET FIGHTERS CIRCLING.

EXT. BAHIA DE LA HABANA - 2 PM

The CASTLE BY THE SEA stands onshore on BERTHA's starboard
side. POV Passengers on deck are looking at the Havana
harbor as BERTHA slowly moves in. She is following a pilot
boat.

MATT is guiding BERTHA into port. He sees people gathered on
a pier to his left. The pilot boat turns toward the pier.
KATE sits next to MATT. MIKE is on his nextel.

                         MIKE
                    (to crewman on bow)
          You handle the ropes. Don't let
          them come aboard.

                         CREWMAN
          Roger. Over.

MATT steers into the dock. News people with cameras are
standing around the pier with officials dressed in suits and
some in uniforms.

BERTHA is tied up. The gangway extended. The CUBAN CAPTAIN
walks down the gangway with his crewmen. They are met by
officials.

CAPTAIN'S BRIDGE

MATT is looking at the crowd and watching the motions of the
officials talking with the CUBAN CAPTAIN.

                         MATT
          I hope I am doing the right thing
          here.

                         KATE
               Don't worry, you did.

                         MIKE
               She is right ole' buddy. If the
               Cuban sticks to his story we'll be
               out of here in no time at all.

                         MATT
               Mike, have a case of our finest
               sent up to the deck. I'll take it
               to the President.

                         MIKE
               Good idea.

MIKE leaves the bridge. A limousine sits back on the pier in
the crowd of people. Kate points to the limo.

                         KATE
               Matt, look.

                         MATT
               There's our ride. I may need an
               interpreter. Wanna go?

                         KATE
               I wouldn't miss it for the world.

MATT sees the CUBAN CAPTAIN coming up the gangway.

                         MATT
               I think the verdict is in Kate.
               Here he comes.

ON DECK

JAKE and NADINE are looking at the large crowd of people on
the pier as the CUBAN CAPTAIN boards and walks to the bridge
steps.

                         NADINE
               These Cubans really like to welcome
               their folks home don't they
               darlin"?

                         JAKE
               Yea. I wonder what kind of food
               they got here. I'm starvin'.

CUBAN CAPTAIN enters the bridge. He looks at MATT.

                         CUBAN CAPTAIN
                      (Spanish)
               The captain and crew will be
               welcomed to Havana as heroes. The
               President assures you there will be
               no problems and conveys his best
               wishes. A representative will meet
               you on the pier to discuss the
               day's planned activities.

                         MATT
               Kate, what did he say?

Kate interprets.

                         KATE
               Are you ready to meet the President
               of Cuba?

                         MATT
               Let's do it.

MATT leaves the bridge with KATE and the CUBAN CAPTAIN. They
descend the steps to the deck and meet MIKE.

                         MIKE
               The case of jars is ready to move
               off the boat. Just signal me when
               the time is right.

                         MATT
               We'll be back. Keep BERTHA safe.
               OK.

                         MIKE
               No problem. Go on now.

HAVANA PIER

MATT and KATE walk down the gangway . They meet the Cuban
representative on the pier.

                         CUBAN REP
                      (in English)
               Welcome to Cuba

He shakes MATT'S hand.

                         CUBAN REP (cont'd)
               Your people are also welcome. If
               you please, we have planned a
               joyful day for them at the Hotel
                         (MORE)

                    CUBAN REP (cont'd)
          Nacional de Cuba. A limousine is
          waiting to take you for lunch with
          our President.

                    MATT
          I would like to take my interpreter
          with me . Is that alright?

                    CUBAN REP
          Of course.

MATT turns to KATE and back to the CUBAN REP.

                    MATT
          This is my interpreter, Kate
          Beauregard.

The CUBAN REP bows (slightly) and shakes her hand.

                    CUBAN REP
          It is very nice to meet you.

                    KATE
          Thank you. Nice to meet you.

                    CUBAN REP
          Shall I show you to the limousine?

                    MATT
          Hold on just a minute.

MATT turns and walks up the gangway. On deck he stands in
front of the passengers aboard.

                    MATT (cont'd)
          These folks want to take you to the
          HOTEL NACIONAL .I think it is an
          exclusive place. Anybody
          interested.

The AC moves next to MATT.

                    AC
          Please follow me if your
          interested. I will speak with the
          Cuban representative to coordinate.

The crowd of passengers move down the gangway. JOHN and
MADDIE follow. MADDIE surveys the crowd of people and
journalist standing on the dock.

                    MADDIE
          John, the Hotel Nacional is written
          about as one of the most refined
          hotels in Cuba. I think the decor
          is 1930s vintage. Sounds
          interesting.

                    JOHN
          I'm sure it is nice. Your daughter
          is going to meet the dictator of
          Cuba. Does that also strike you as
          interesting?

MADDIE looks at JOHN. They walk toward the crowd. KATE
approaches MADDIE and JOHN.

                    KATE
          I'll meet you back here later. Have
          a good time and don't worry.

She kisses both parents and walks away.

BEN and JENNY are met by an American journalist with camera
man.

                    JOURNALIST
          Hello. Could I have a word with
          you.

                    BEN
          You need to make it quick. We are
          leaving.

They are walking along as the journalist reaches out with
the microphone and the camera man backs up pointing his lens
at the two.

                    JOURNALIST
          What happened at sea. Did your
          captain really rescue the Cubans?

                    JENNY
          Are you an idiot? We brought them
          here didn't we? What a stupid
          question Ben.

                    BEN
          No comment. We need to go now.Thank
          you very much.

BEN and JENNY move away from the journalist. The journalist
turns to catch another passenger. JAKE is walking past the
journalist and is stopped.

                                          (CONTINUED)

                         JOURNALIST
                Sir, can you say exactly what
                happened out there today?

                         JAKE
                Sure I can. How hard would that be.

JAKE walks away. Buses are lined up along the pier tarmac.
Passengers are boarding the buses. Off to the left of the
buses sits a black limo with an official seal on the side
passenger door.MATT and KATE are escorted to the limo. MATT
reaches for his nextel.

                         MATT
                Mike,over.

                         MIKE
                Yes. Go ahead.

                         MATT
                I almost forgot the brew. Can you
                get it here quick before we leave.

                         MIKE
                I'll send it right now. Over.

A driver opens the rear door. KATE enters the car. MATT
follows her. A courier runs up to the limo and opens the
trunk . He places the box of moonshine in the trunk. The
trunk lid shuts. The passenger door shuts. The driver gets
in and shuts his door. The limo moves away from the pier.

INT. LIMOUSINE - DAY 45 MINUTES LATER

KATE is leaning forward in her seat and looking through the
tinted window.

                         KATE
                Wow. look ahead at that.

A view of the FINCA PRESIDENTIAL COMPOUND.

                         MATT
                Looks like a fortress, but the
                grounds are beautiful.

The limo turns into a long driveway. Up ahead, a well
dressed young man stands at the large mahogany side entry
doors. The limo swings around and under a canopy and comes
to a stop. The doorman opens the limo door. KATE exits
followed by MATT. The driver opens the trunk and hands a box
to another person at the entrance to the compound. KATE and

MATT disappear behind the mahogany doors as they swing
closed.

INT. FINCA PRESIDENTIAL COMPOUND - DAY

MATT and KATE are escorted down a hallway of hardwood floors
and paneling into a formal dining room. A waiter seats them.
The dining room table is rectangular and made of cherry. A
woman dressed in a black and white servants outfit comes
through a side entry door carrying a silver tray. On it sits
three mason jars with moonshine in them. Matt looks up.

                    MATT
          You can tell this one to your
          grandchildren.

                    KATE
          Our grandchildren.

A young man in uniform swings open a door behind the dining
area and the President walks through. He walks straight to
the table. MATT stands up. The President offers his hand to
MATT. They shake hands.

                    EL PRESIDENTE
               (Spanish)
          Welcome sir. Thank you for coming
          on such short notice.

KATE interprets. Matt looks at her and then the President.

                    MATT
          No problem.

KATE looks at MATT.

                    KATE
          Is that it?

                    MATT
          What else?

                    KATE
          OK.

Kate interprets to the President. He walks over and leans
down. He kisses her hand.

                    EL PRESIDENTE
          What a beautiful flower has
          arrived. Thank you for coming.

                         KATE
              Gracias, senor Presidente.

EL PRESIDENTE is seated. MATT sits down. The servants bring
in the entrees. The meal is served. El PRESIDENTE raises a
jar of moonshine. MATT and KATE raise their jars.

                      EL PRESIDENTE
              A toast to you for your kind
              service to our country.

KATE interprets.

MATT sips the drink. KATE sips her drink. El PRESIDENTE
watches as they drink the moonshine down.(PAUSE). He looks
at the jar and smiles. He then takes a drink.

                 EL PRESIDENTE (cont'd)
              Whooh! Es muy bueno! Mas.

He takes another drink.

                 EL PRESIDENTE (cont'd)
                   (Spanish)
              This is fine whiskey. Did you
              produce this?

Kate interprets all.

                         MATT
              Yes. It is called moonshine.

                      EL PRESIDENTE
              La Luna Brillante!

He takes another drink and sets the jar down.

                 EL PRESIDENTE (cont'd)
              Captain, would you consider a
              business proposal?

MATT AND KATE look at each other.

EXT. HOTEL NACIONAL DE CUBA - AFTERNOON

JAKE is buried to his neck in sand. JJ and JENELLA finish
packing the sand around his neck. JJ puts a round straw hat
on JAKE'S head as a jet ski (ZOOMS) past. JENELLA and JJ
turn to look. NADINE is close by lying in the sun.

                                              (CONTINUED)

ROY KELLER, an older man, and his wife are riding the jet
ski close to shore. The wife is going very fast and loses
control. A wave drives the jet ski into shore beaching it .
ROY is launched over her head and into the beach.JAKE looks
over at JJ and JENELLA.

                        JAKE
            Go help the old man up .

NADINE lays her head sideways toward JAKE.

                        NADINE
            Are you comfortable now.

                        JAKE
            The sand is cooler down below
            around my feet.

A (FAT WOMAN) in bathing suit with male companion walk by .
She reaches for her sandal to remove debris and loses her
balance. She falls backward over JAKE'S head barely missing
it and (SLAMS) her rear end down hard on the sand. (WHOOSH).

JAKE'S straw hat is pinned to his ears by her enormous
thighs. His face pointed directly at her crotch.The FAT
WOMAN looks down and sees JAKES eyes beneath the rim of the
hat. He is staring into her crotch. She (SCREAMS).

                        FAT WOMAN
            You pervert.

JJ and JENELLA arrive in time to pull the woman's feet up
and over the FAT WOMAN causing her to roll backwards into
the ocean. NADINE looks on.

                        NADINE
                  (to JJ and JENELLA)
            Dig him out of there right now.

CUT TO:

Above the beach stands the HOTEL NACIONAL. JOHN AND MADDIE
sit sipping drinks in a cabana. A waiter hands them fresh
drinks.

Behind them on a terrace paved with stones BEN and JENNY
look out into the sea. Dolphins are swimming by in pairs
close to shore.

                        JENNY
            Look, dolphins.

                    BEN
          According to Science Magazine, a
          well known marine biologist stated
          that sharks are now able to mimic
          the swimming patterns and sounds
          made by dolphins. In this way they
          can lure unsuspecting dolphin
          lovers into the water.

                    JENNY
          Are you serious.

                    BEN
          No.(laughs)

JENNY strikes BEN on the shoulder. He moves to a set of
steps to the beach and looks back at her. She follows. He
kicks off his shoes and runs. She runs after him passing by
JOHN and MADDIE'S cabana. JOHN notices the two running.

                    JOHN
          Maddie, remember those days?

                    MADDIE
          We're just as good, just not as
          fast.

                    JOHN
          Let's go swimming in the sea.

                    MADDIE
          I can swim about as well as that
          ape playing with the children down
          there.

She points to FRANK. (ZOOM IN ON FRANK). FRANK is standing
in knee deep water with a diving mask over his hairy face.
He is bent over looking into the ocean water.

(VIEW OF FISH IN THE WATER).   FADE OUT

INT. FINCA PRESIDENTIAL COMPOUND - LATER

MATT is looking directly at KATE across the dining table.
She then turns her head toward El PRESIDENTE.

                    KATE
          Do you think he will be alright? He
          hasn't said a word in 30 seconds.
          Should we call someone?

The camera (PANS) over to the president. His face is frozen.
A cigar between his lips , burned down to within an inch of
his lips with ashes barely clinging to the cigar . His left
eyelid is almost closed. His right eye is wide open. He is
sitting up straight and is not moving.

                    MATT
          No. He will be OK in a few more
          seconds. It is a form of brain
          freeze when your body suddenly
          tells your brain you just drank too
          much moonshine. I do hope that
          cigar is not burning. He could
          potentially explode.

KATE stands up and moves close to EL PRESIDENTE and takes
the cigar gently from his mouth placing it in a small glass
ashtray next to him. She then puts her fingers on his neck
to check for a pulse.

                    KATE
          He is alive alright.I will go call
          the waiter and tell him we wish to
          leave. You can stay here until I
          get back. I think EL PRESIDENTE
          needs a nap.

The moonshine jar sits empty next to EL PRESIDENTE. A view
of his face.

EXT. HOTEL NACIONAL DE CUBA - LATE AFTERNOON

JAKE is lying beside NADINE in the afternoon sun. Children
playing all around. JJ AND JENELLA approach JAKE.

                    JENELLA
          Daddy, look up there. Do you see
          that guy way up there hanging from
          that parachute?

JAKE makes his hand into a hat bill and raises up
(SQUINTING) his eyes.

                    JAKE
          Ain't that somethin'?

                    NADINE
          Why don't you show us how it's done
          baby?

                    JAKE
          Get that instamatic camera ready.
          I'm gone.

JAKE rises off the sand and walks to a beach shack. He pays
for a para sail ride. NADINE loads the camera while the kids
run to catch up with JAKE.

MADDIE AND JOHN are nodding off under the cabana. JOHN hears
someone nearby talking.

                    TOURIST
          Isn't that one of our passengers
          getting a parachute harness
          strapped on?

A muffled answer comes back. JOHN sits up in the chair and
looks at JAKE as he is running toward the water with the tow
rope pulling him off the beach.

JAKE is off out over the surf. Close up shot.

                    JAKE
          Who's your daddy now ?

NADINE sees JAKE rising fast.

                    NADINE
          Watch him soar like an eagle kids.
          That's my man!

                    JJ
          Momma, he's goin' awful high up.

The boat speeds away . JAKE rises to 350 feet. The boat
turns down the coast. The para sail grows smaller then the
boat turns back up the coast. The boat driver grounds on the
beach as he closes in to the landing area in front of the
SPARKS family.

JAKE sees the rope slack as the boat stops. The para sail
drifts freely . JAKE looks up. The sail collapses. He
corkscrews down, spiraling into the water.

A young teenaged Cuban LIFEGUARD jumps from his stand and
runs full blast into the water as the sail falls on top of
JAKE. He reaches the sail and dives under looking for JAKE.
JAKE is thrashing around and struggling to stay above water.
The sail sinking around him.

NADINE and the children are running into the water as the
LIFEGUARD looks for JAKE.

Underneath the sail and sinking, JAKE panics. The young
LIFEGUARD sees him below the surface and moves fast to reach
JAKE.

The LIFEGUARD struggles to pull JAKE from under the sail as
JAKE inhales sea water. The LIFEGUARD pulls JAKE out from
under the sail and to the surface.

NADINE and the children arrive to help the LIFEGUARD pull
JAKE up while treading water. They pull JAKE to the beach
and lay him on his back. The LIFEGUARD performs CPR. JAKE is
revived as NADINE, JJ AND JENELLA look on. A crowd of people
surround them. NADINE moves close to JAKES face as he is
spewing and gasping to clear his lungs.

                         NADINE
               Jake, can you hear me. Wake up now.

JAKE opens his eyes and looks at NADINE.

                         JAKE
                    (barely audible)
               I told you I could do it. Did you
               get any good shots.

                         NADINE
               Yes darlin', I snapped a good one
               just before you hit the water.

JAKE smiles weakly. He is helped up on his feet by the Cuban
LIFEGUARD.

                         LIFEGUARD
                    (English)
               Sir, are you going to be alright.
               We can take you to a hospital if
               you wish.

                         JAKE
               That ain't necessary young man,
               but I owe you for saving my life
               son.

JAKE is standing looking at the LIFEGUARD then stumbles
forward a few steps.

                         LIFEGUARD
               This is my job sir. Please , you
               owe me nothing. I am happy you are
               well.

                         JAKE
              No. I was a goner and you risked
              your life for me.

The young LIFEGUARD surveys the crowd.

                         LIFEGUARD
              Please everyone. It is over now.
              Everything is fine. The gentleman
              needs some room to breath. Please
              make way.

LIFEGUARD puts him arm around JAKE and leads him up to the
beach area as NADINE goes for a beach towel. They help JAKE
to sit down on the towel. The LIFEGUARD stands in front of
the SPARKS family sitting around JAKE.

                         JAKE
              If you ever visit Kentucky, we will
              consider you a special guest and
              friend for life.

                         LIFEGUARD
              If it were possible to leave Cuba,
              I would do so, however we are
              forbidden to leave.

                         JAKE
              Really, why.

                         LIFEGUARD
              It is the law. I have tried to find
              a way to the United States many
              times. It is not possible without
              much risk.

JAKE looks at NADINE as he wipes his face with a towel.

                         JAKE
              I have an idea.

                         NADINE
              Oh no. Don't even think about it.

                         JAKE
              No. Listen. I know how we can make
              his dreams come true.

                         NADINE
              Jake, I can see it in your eyes and
              we will never get away with it.

                         JAKE
          We have to try. This young man
          risked it all for me.

JENELLA is looking at the LIFEGUARD

                         JENELLA
          What is your name?

                         LIFEGUARD
          Enrico. Yours?

                         JENELLA
          Jenella

JENELLA smiles at ENRICO.

                         JAKE
          Your name is Rick from now on. We
          are going to take you home with us.
          Would you like that son?

                         ENRICO
          How is that possible?

                         JAKE
          Just leave it to me. Here, sit down
          for a minute while we get things
          worked out. When do you go off
          duty?

ENRICO sits down.

                         ENRICO
          I am off duty in a few minutes.

                         JAKE
          We are going to be back at the boat
          at six tonight.

                         NADINE
          It's four right now.

JAKE hesitates for a moment.

                         JAKE
          Son, do you have family you need to
          talk to about this?

                         ENRICO
          Just my grandmother. She lives with
          my aunt. My parents are deceased.

                    JAKE
          You go tell your grandma what you
          want to do and meet us back here in
          one hour. Don't be late and bring
          only a few things so no one will be
          suspicious. I will work out the
          plan while your gone.

                    ENRICO
          Thank you very much. I must go now.

ENRICO walks toward the hotel ..

JAKE looks at NADINE and the kids.

                    JAKE
          Listen. This is what we will do.

EXT. DOCKSIDE 6 PM DAY

The limo pulls up to the pier. MATT and KATE exit the
vehicle. The tour buses are parked in a row nearby.
Passengers are leaving the buses and heading for the pier.

News people are gathered on the pier. MATT sees KATE's
parents. He points them out to her.

                    MATT
          There they are.

KATE sees them and walks toward them as MATT is approached
by an American news reporter.

                    AMERICAN NEWS REPORTER
          Captain, could I have a word with
          you?

A microphone and camera are pushed in his face.

                    MATT
          Make it quick. I need to cast off
          immediately.

                    REPORTER
          The American public is watching
          this story. Do you have any
          comment?

                    MATT
          I haven't really had time to think
          about it yet.

                    REPORTER
          Did you meet the President of Cuba
          today?

                    MATT
          We did and were given permission to
          leave, which is what I intend to do
          right now, thank you.

MATT spots MIKE in the crowd.

                    MATT (cont'd)
          Gotta go. Thanks.

A courier approaches the gangway with a box. He hands it off
to the purser and leaves. The box is carried up to the
bridge and placed inside.

Reporters surround the passengers as they move toward
BERTHA. MIKE and MATT find each other.

                    MIKE
          Hey boy, where you been all day?

                    MATT
          I'll tell you later. Let's get her
          out of here.

MATT moves through the crowd and up the gangway. MIKE
follows. FRANK is (scampering) up the bridge steps ahead of
them.

The AC stands next to the gangway with a clipboard. He is
checking off the manifest of passengers. Next to him is a
Cuban official observing the passengers passing by. He keeps
his eyes on the checklist.

JAKE,NADINE,JJ,JENELLA AND ENRICO approach the gangway. JAKE
staggers from side to side as he walks up to the AC.

                    JAKE
               (slurring speech)
          Howdy, everybody. Viva la Cuber and
          all that.

NADINE follows JAKE. She turns to JJ and Enrico.

                    NADINE
          Boys, get your daddy on that boat
          and I mean right now!

JAKE staggers into the Cuban official knocking him backward.
The boys reach for JAKE holding him. They put their
shoulders under JAKE'S arms pulling him along up the
gangway.

The AC checks them off the list as the Cuban adjusts his
clothing. Other passengers follow closely behind.

CAPTAIN'S BRIDGE

MATT sits at the wheel as MIKE moves toward FRANK who is
attempting to open the box on the floor.

                    MIKE
          Hold on Frank, what you got there.

                    MATT
          What's that box doing there.

MIKE opens the box. It is full of Cuban cigars and a letter
addressed to MATT. MIKE hands the letter to MATT.

                    MIKE
          It appears you made a friend.

                    MATT
          What do you mean?

MIKE hands a cigar to MATT and gives one to FRANK.

                    MATT (cont'd)
          I reckon the old man favored us .
          He gave us some fine cigars.

MATT puts the envelope in his pocket.

                    MATT (cont'd)
          Light em' up boys.

EXT. BERTHA OUT TO SEA 6:45 PM

The sun is setting off to port side as BERTHA moves out of
Havana Harbor. Passengers are milling around the deck areas.

MATT steers BERTHA out to sea. (View of stern with wake)

INT. BERTHA - SUNSET

MATT,MIKE AND FRANK are smoking cigars.

                    MATT
          Our ETA ST.Thomas is sunrise about
          12 hours if the seas cooperate.

                    MIKE
          Good news. The GPS is working
          again.

                    MATT
          It doesn't get much better than
          this.

BERTHA (SURGES) FORWARD . THE COASTLINE DISAPPEARS.

NIGHTLY NEWS CNC NEW YORK 6:50 PM

Tight on NEWS ANCHOR.

                    ANCHOR
          And now an update on the events in
          Cuba today. The American cruise
          ship, BERTHA, sailed from Havana
          this evening. CNC reports the
          captain met with the Cuban
          president after the reported rescue
          of Cuban naval personnel. The
          longstanding trade embargo, a
          highly controversial issue in
          Washington today, may well be
          revisited after the goodwill
          efforts of the Cuban president as
          well as the American captain show
          promise for a more conciliatory
          atmosphere between the two nations.
          We will keep you up to date on this
          hot button topic. And now....

INT. BERTHA - EVENING 9 PM

JAKE sits in the cabin with his family and Enrico.

                    JAKE
          Looks like I might need to go see
          the captain about Enrico since we
          are out of Cuban territory now.

(CONTINUED)

                         ENRICO
               Does this mean I am free Mr.
               Sparks.

                         JAKE
               So far so good. Long as nobody in
               Cuba gets wind of this, you are
               going to be fine.

                         NADINE
               Jake, how do you suppose the
               captain will act about this?

                         JAKE
               I reckon I better go see him now.

JAKE gets up and walks out of the cabin.

INT. BERTHA - EVENING 9 PM

JAKE knocks on the bridge door. MIKE answers.

                         JAKE
               Good evenin' sir. Could I speak
               with the captain for a minute?

                         MIKE
               Sure, come in. Who should I say you
               are?

                         JAKE
               Jake Sparks.

MIKE turns toward MATT at the wheel.

                         MIKE
               Captain, you got a visitor.

                         MATT
               OK. What can I do for you?

MATT turns to see JAKE.

                         JAKE
               Howdy.

                         MATT
               Come on in.

                         JAKE
               Thanks.

MATT leaves the wheel to MIKE.

                    MATT
          You want to step outside for a
          minute, get some fresh air?

                    JAKE
          Fine.

They leave the bridge and step onto the steel platform
outside near the stair railing. MATT looks at JAKE.

                    MATT
          Yes sir. What is it. Everything
          goin' alright for you tonight?

                    JAKE
          I brought a Cuban with us back to
          the boat. He is in my cabin. He
          saved my life today on the beach. I
          owe him. He wanted to get to the
          states. So, that's it.

MATT stares into JAKE'S eyes.

                    MATT
          A Cuban? Who is this Cuban?

                    JAKE
          Enrico.

                    MATT
          So, Enrico saves your life and
          wants to be an American?

                    JAKE
          Yes sir, that's right.

                    MATT
          You know he is now a liability. He
          will have to pass through
          immigration back in Mobile? And,
          how in the hell did you get him on
          board?

                    JAKE
          That was the easy part. I just
          wanted you to know so that we could
          work something out for the boy. He
          deserves a break.

MATT (pauses). He looks out to sea.

                    MATT
          Does he have family in Cuba?

                    JAKE
          Just a grandma.

                    MATT
          OK.

                    JAKE
          Look sir, I didn't want anybody
          knowin' this except for you. I hope
          we can keep it that way. He almost
          looks American anyway and speaks
          American real good.

MATT looks at JAKE (SMILING)

                    MATT
          You are quite a man to do this.
          Sure, we can keep it to ourselves.I
          will hire him as a crewman when we
          get to ST. Thomas. Meanwhile, keep
          him in your cabin. Anything else?

                    JAKE
          Nope, that's about all.

MATT reaches out and shakes JAKE'S hand.

                    MATT
          Alright, you have a nice evening
          Mr. Sparks.

INT. BERTHA NIGHT 9:30PM

A crowd is dancing and dining in the great hall as MATT
walks in. He sees JOHN and MADDIE sitting at a table
drinking. He approaches them.

                    MATT
          Good evening folks. Are you having
          a good time tonight?

                    JOHN
          Have a seat captain.

MATT sits down at the table.

                    MADDIE
          Are you in love with my daughter?

MADDIE takes another drink.

                         JOHN
               Maddie, can't you see the captain
               has had a long day. He probably
               needs a drink. How about it
               captain?

JOHN takes another drink. His eyes are glazed. MADDIE
finishes her drink quickly.

                         MADDIE
               Yes darling, you do look tired.
               Please join us . John , get the boy
               a drink.

                         JOHN
               Garcon (laughs).

John waves for a waitress.

                         MATT
               Have you seen Kate?

                         MADDIE
               I asked you. Are you in love with
               our daughter?

                         MATT
               Well, Mrs. Beauregard...

                         JOHN
               Maddie, hush up now. This boy is
               doing his best to run this ship
               properly. Let him be.

                         MADDIE
               John T. Beauregard, don't you even
               think about bossing me around, I
               will kick your ass kind sir.

MATT listens to the exchange.

                         JOHN
               My dear wife, I will not tolerate
               such insolence or whatever the hell
               that means. Matt this woman has
               been my wife for over 35 years and
               has never talked to me like that.
               Well, maybe once when I lost Kate
               at the Houston zoo.

                         MATT
               Look folks, I can have someone get
               you drinks and help you to your
                         (MORE)

                    MATT (cont'd)
          room if you want. I need to leave
          now. How about it?

                    JOHN
          Good idea. We need to go up to the
          cabin and rest for awhile. Come on
          Maddie let's get out of here.

                    MATT
          Alright, have a good evening.

MATT heads for the elevator. The door opens. KATE is
standing in front of him.

                    MATT (cont'd)
          Our grandchildren

                    KATE
          Excuse me?

                    MATT
          You said our grandchildren not your
          grandchildren. I mean you said you
          would tell our grandchildren.You
          did not say I would tell my
          grandchildren.

                    KATE
          Now I am really confused. Just what
          are you talking about?

                    MATT
          You know what I am talking about.
          Just forget I mentioned it. I am
          going to go up and get some sleep.
          By the way, your parents are
          hammered. You should see about
          them.

                    KATE
          My parents are perfectly capable of
          taking care of themselves. So, when
          you figure out what you are talking
          about let me know.

KATE walks past MATT toward the main hall. MATT enters the
elevator. The doors close. KATE finds her parents talking at
the table.

                    KATE (cont'd)
          What are you two doing now?

                         MADDIE
              You are in love with that sailor
              boy aren't you dear?

                         KATE
              Mom, what is going on here? Dad,
              why is she acting this way?

                         JOHN
              Don't worry baby, we were just
              reminiscing . Maddie, let's go up
              to bed now.

                         MADDIE
              Yes dear, why did I not think of
              that.

INT. BERTHA - NIGHT

KATE is knocking on MATT'S cabin door.The door opens.

                         KATE
              Did you figure out what you meant?

MATT pulls KATE into his cabin. The door shuts.

INT. BERTHA - NIGHT

BEN is lying on his bed. JENNY beside him. Both fully
clothed.

                         BEN
              Let's play the do ya game

                         JENNY
              What's that?

                         BEN

Simple. I ask you a question beginning with do ya and you
answer yes or no. You then ask me a question. No repeat
questions.You go first.

                         JENNY
              Do you pick your nose in public?

                         BEN
              No. Do you like to keep you house
              spotless all the time?

                         JENNY
               No. Do you fart in bed?

                         BEN
               No. Do you snore?

                         JENNY
               No. Do you chew your food with your
               mouth open?

                         BEN
               No. Do you like candlelight
               dinners?

                         JENNY
               Yes. Do you like drinking a nice
               glass of wine after dinner in the
               cold winter time while lying naked
               on a rug in front of a burning
               fireplace with someone special?

                         BEN
               Yes, but you asked way too many
               questions.

BEN reaches for JENNY.

INT. BEN'S CABIN 5 AM NEXT MORNING

JENNY and BEN are lying face to face on the bed. JENNY is
snoring. BEN farts.

EXT. BERTHA. MORNING 6 AM

JAKE is sitting with several early risers in swiveling
fishing chairs on the stern deck. He is looking out to sea.
He is holding a cup of steaming coffee.

A froth of white foam stretches across the horizon.

                         JAKE
                    (to man next to him)
               Look out there. You got any
               binoculars?

                         MAN NUMBER ONE
               Yes. Right here.

He hands them to JAKE.

                                                     (CONTINUED)

                         MAN NUMBER TWO
               I see what you're talkin' about.
               There is something out there.

     JAKE is looking through the binoculars. He scans the
     horizon.

                         JAKE
               It looks like a ridge of water
               comin' this way and we're goin'
               pretty fast as it is.

                         MAN NUMBER ONE
               I think we need to tell the
               captain.

     JAKE jumps down off the chair.

                         JAKE
               I'll be back in a minute. You boys
               keep an eye on her.

     JAKE trots to the forward deck area and runs up the stairs
     to the bridge. He knocks on the door.

     Mike answers.

                         MIKE
               Hello there again. What's going on
               this morning?

                         JAKE
               Is the captain around?

                         MIKE
               What's up?

                         JAKE
               There's somethin' mighty strange
               chasin' after us back yonder. Looks
               like a white foam ridge.You better
               get the captain.

                         MIKE
               Show me.

     MIKE steps out onto the stair landing with JAKE and reaches
     for his nextel.

                         MIKE (cont'd)
               Captain, you are needed on the
               bridge asap. Over

                    MATT
          Roger. Be there in a minute.

JAKE points to the horizon. MIKE grabs a pair of binoculars.
He sees the long white ridge of foam

                    MIKE
          You're right. There is something
          strange happening out there.
          Captain will be here in a minute.
          Thanks for the heads up.

                    JAKE
          Right.

JAKE descends the steps and trots back to his fishing chair
as the others sit looking out to sea.

                    JAKE (cont'd)
          Reckon what that is boys?

                    MAN NUMBER TWO
          I think it is one of them runaway
          waves I seen on National Geographic
          one time.

                    JAKE
          Well, if that's true we are in for
          it unless we can outrun it.

INT. BERTHA'S BRIDGE - MORNING 6:09 AM

MATT enters the bridge. MIKE is waiting for him.

                    MIKE
          Come here.

They step out onto the stair landing. Both looking aft to
the horizon. MATT is using binoculars.

                    MATT
          It is a rogue wave. We need to move
          fast. What is our speed.

                    MIKE
          30 knots

                    MATT
          Full speed ahead. Now.

MIKE leaps toward the bridge door. He moves to the wheel and
pushes the throttle wide open. BERTHA surges forward.

                                           (CONTINUED)

On the rear deck JAKE and his companions are jolted by the
thrust of the boat and see the wake surge outward.

                    JAKE
          Strap those belts on boys. We are
          in for a ride.

BRIDGE

MATT takes the wheel. FRANK (CHATTERS). MIKE sits down and
looks at the radar scanner.

The second officer uses binoculars and looks rearward
through the window.

                    SECOND OFFICER
          Sir, it is closing fast. It appears
          to be approximately 40 to 50 feet
          high. I can't estimate it's speed.

                    MATT
          How close.

                    SECOND OFFICER
          Quarter mile at most.

                    MATT
          MIKE, we don't have time to alert
          the passengers.

                    MIKE
          I know.

                    MATT
          Is this all we got for speed. I
          need more.

                    MIKE
          You're wide open Matt.

REAR DECK

JAKE and the boys are gripping the chairs.

                    JAKE
          Hang on boys. This is it!

EXT. EXXON OIL TANKER. 6:15 AM

View of oil tanker crossing Bertha's path at an angle.

INT. BERTHA'S BRIDGE - 6:16

MATT and MIKE look straight ahead and see the oil tanker.
The tanker is turning to head into the rogue wave. It is
moving toward BERTHA diagonally.

                    MATT
          When the wave gets close to the
          stern I will reverse thrust and
          back us up on the wave.

                    MIKE
          Why?

                    MATT
          We can't survive the wave going
          over us and the tanker will kill us
          if we don't get above it.

                    MIKE
          That tanker is closing on us fast.

                    MATT
          Just pray we can ride over her.

                    MIKE
          I am praying!

The wave reaches the stern. JAKE and the boys are holding
tight to the chairs. A sudden thrust pushes them against the
backs of the chairs. BERTHA is in reverse and climbing the
wave to the crest.

View of BERTHA riding the wave.

View of the OIL TANKER crossing directly in front of BERTHA.

View of the wave pushing BERTHA into the TANKER bow.

BERTHA rides over the bow of the OIL TANKER and (ZOOMS)
across the deck of the tanker and (SKIMMING) the top of the
deck. BERTHA (GLIDES) down the other side of the tanker
washed by the crest of the breaking wave.

OIL TANKER (CRASHES) at an angle into the brunt of the forty
foot wave.

INT.BERTHA

Passengers tossed around inside cabins. Dining hall wrecked.

BRIDGE - MOMENTS LATER

MATT , MIKE and FRANK sit still as BERTHA rocks in the
water. Showers of sea spray (FLY) over BERTHA. MATT watches
the rogue wave move away from them. BERTHA settles in the
sea and is still.

MATT looks at MIKE.

                    MATT
          We made it. Check the passengers.
          Make sure everyone is OK. I will
          steer around and look for the oil
          tanker.

MIKE leaves the bridge.

AFT DECK

JAKE is staring out to sea as are all the men on the swivel
chairs. They are soaking wet.

                    JAKE
          Thank you Jesus.

INT. BERTHA DINING HALL - 6:20

People are cleaning up the dining hall . Cooks are gathering
items in the kitchen.

BEAUREGARD CABIN

JOHN holds MADDIE. KATE looks through the porthole window.

                    KATE
          What a ride. What in heavens name
          was that?

                    JOHN
          We took an unscheduled trip on a
          wave.

                    MADDIE
          I am going to be sick now.

EXT. OIL TANKER 6:30

The oil tanker steams away unscathed as MATT looks through
his binoculars at it. He turns and goes back onto the
bridge. He sits at the wheel and turns the boat hard around
slowly. He looks over at the second officer.

                    MATT
          Take the wheel and set course for
          ST. Thomas. Set cruising speed at
          45 knots. I need to check the
          passengers.

He leaves the bridge.

INT. BERTHA DINING HALL - 6:45

Passengers milling around. Some eating. The sounds of people
talking (LOUDLY). KATE walks into the dining hall with MATT.
MATT reaches for a microphone.

                    MATT
          Folks, it appears everyone made it
          through without injury. Thank God
          for that. We are still on schedule
          to be in ST. Thomas today. Thanks.

He looks at KATE.

NADINE is standing at the buffet with To Go Boxes. She is
filling them with breakfast food. JAKE is holding some of
the boxes.

BEN and JENNY are sitting at a table drinking orange juice.

                    JENNY
          Were we almost killed this morning?
          Should I be glad that I took this
          cruise? Have we had anything but
          trouble the whole time?

BEN looks at her (hesitates)

                    BEN
          I would not have met you if you
          hadn't taken this cruise. I think
          it is well worth the trip.

JENNY leans over and kisses BEN.

EXT. ST. THOMAS . DAY 1 PM

A view of BERTHA approaching the harbor. People on board moving around the deck.

A group of reporters are standing at the dock with cameras and locals.

Blue skies and a light breeze warm the passengers on the deck of BERTHA.

INT. BERTHA . SAME

JAKE sits in his cabin with the family and ENRICO. JAKE looks at ENRICO.

                    JAKE
          Son, you should stay here in the
          cabin until we get back. I will
          have the captain come up to meet
          you. He will take you ashore.

                    NADINE
          There is plenty of food in the
          refrigerator.

                    JENELLA
          I wish you could go with us.

                    JJ
          Yea.

                    JAKE
          Don't leave the cabin until I come
          to get you and don't answer the
          door unless it is the captain. Keep
          it locked. You got that son.

                    ENRICO
          Yes sir. I will do as you say.
          Thank you for helping me.

                    JAKE
          I'm glad to .

EXT. BERTHA - LATER

A crowd of passengers move down the gangway and onto the pier. The gathering reporters shove for position.

JAKE passes by MATT standing at the head of the gangway.

                    JAKE
          How ya doin' captain?

                    MATT
          Hello Jake.

                    JAKE
          Fine. Listen, the boy is in our
          cabin. He will stay there until you
          come up to get him after all the
          hub bub is over with the reporters
          and all.

                    MATT
          I will speak with him tonight when
          everybody is on shore. I think it
          would be a good idea to wait until
          dark before we let him go ashore.

                    JAKE
          Yea. Maybe that would be a good
          idea. OK. Well, I'm gonna go now.

                    MATT
          Hey, would you like to play a round
          of golf this afternoon.

                    JAKE
          Sure. Sounds good to me.

                    MATT
          Why don't you find someone to play
          with us. Mike is my partner. Can
          you find another fellow.

                    JAKE
          I think so. I'll ask around.

                    MATT
          Alright. Get back to me .

                    JAKE
          See you this afternoon. Thanks.

JAKE moves down the gangway and joins his family.

KATE follows JOHN and MADDIE walking toward the gangway.
They are dressed for the beach. KATE is holding FRANK'S hand
as some young people follow her.

                    KATE
          You guys stay with me. We have to
          catch a ride to the beach for
          snorkeling.

KATE sees MATT and waves to him. She moves closer.

> KATE (cont'd)
> You're gonna miss a good time.

> MATT
> I'll catch up later. Gonna play
> golf.

> KATE
> You deserve it. I'll see you later.

> MATT
> That's a promise.

KATE moves down into the crowd.

A reporter moves in and puts his microphone in JAKE'S face.

> REPORTER
> Sir, what are your comments
> regarding the incident in Cuba.

> JAKE
> Boy, you fellows really get around.
> The incident, as you call it, was a
> case of miscalculation on the part
> of the driver. I don't fault him
> for droppin' me in the water like
> that. Besides, Nadine got a shot or
> two in for the family album.

The REPORTER stands motionless. His head turns around
looking at the crowd. JAKE walks past him.

A group of teenagers surround a tall figure with a cowboy
hat . He is moving through the crowd toward BERTHA.

MATT sees the last passenger off the gangway and motions to
MIKE.

> MIKE
> What's the plan now.

> MATT
> Come here and look at this.

He points to the man with the cowboy hat on.

> MATT (cont'd)
> You know who that is?

                    MIKE
          Looks like a celebrity. Who is it?

                    MATT
          That, my friend, is Kasey Hays.

                    MIKE
          No way.

                    MATT
          Sure is.

                    MIKE
          By the way, I let the crew have the
          day off. I told them to be back
          tonight. If anybody needs a meal
          later on we will open up the
          kitchen.

                    MATT
          Alright, let's go.

KASEY HAYS meets MATT at the bottom of the gangway.

                    KASEY
          Hey there captain.

                    MATT
          Hi. You are Kasey Hays, right?

                    KASEY
          Yep. You are the captain right?

                    MATT
          You got it. Nice to meet you. I'm a
          fan of yours.

                    KASEY
          I appreciate that.

They shake hands.

                    KASEY (cont'd)
          Hey captain, do you think you and
          the crew and passengers would mind
          if I gave them a little party
          tonight ? Just my way of saying
          thanks for all us American folks
          who appreciate what you did for
          those Cuban boys.

                         MATT
          I'm sure most of them would pay
          just to see you perform. Yes, we
          would really be thrilled to have
          you do something. What time and
          where?

                         KASEY
          How about right here on the pier? I
          believe we can arrange to use this
          space with the locals. Tell you
          what, we'll just have a good ole
          time, cook a little and play a
          little. How's about eight 8
          tonight?

                         MATT
          Sounds good to me.

                         KASEY
          It was a honor meetin' you captain.
          I'll be seein' you tonight.

They shake hands. KASEY turns away with a host of reporters
and fans around him.

MATT looks over at MIKE.

                         MATT
          Can you believe that?

                         MIKE
          It's a party tonight.

CAMERA SHOWS ENRICO LOOKING OUT PORTHOLE WINDOW . SAME

EXT. GOLF COURSE. DAY

JAKE is standing at the first tee. His partner behind him, a
6'8" man dressed in overalls with a slingshot in his back
pocket.

JAKE swings and misses. He swings again. The ball hits his
golf cart and bounces around.

His partner tees up. He hits the ball straight and out of
sight.

MIKE tees off short and straight. MATT tees off and hooks.

MATT looks over at JAKE near the golf cart.

                                               (CONTINUED)

JAKE hits his third ball fifty yards.

                    MATT
          Hey Jake, what's the slingshot for?

                    JAKE
          When he first started playin' he
          hit in the rough a lot. He says the
          flipper rounded up a lot of small
          game while he was learnin' to play.

                    MATT
          OH.

                    MIKE
          Did you see that drive the big
          fellow made.

                    MATT
          We may be in trouble.

FIFTH TEE

JAKE rips the ground up. He repeats it three times. The ball
goes ten yards.

His partner drives the ball straight out of sight again.

6TH HOLE SANDTRAP

JAKE is OV in the sandtrap. Sand flys out. Again. The ball
lands on the edge of the sandtrap and rolls back down. JAKE
sprays sand again.

GREEN

JAKE putts long . The ball rolls off the green . He repeats
the long putts off the green twice more.

MIKE, MATT and PARTNER stand beside the golf carts. JAKE
hits another putt long past the hole and off the green.

7TH tee

JAKE'S PARTNER launches a rocket ball onto the green next to
the hole. The others (stare) in amazement.

9TH HOLE 140 YARDS.

Three successive drives are seen, MIKE,MATT,THE PARTNER.

JAKE drives the ball over the green into the clubhouse
window and inside the clubhouse. View of ball bouncing
around inside the clubhouse.

EXT. BEACH. SAME

FRANK is standing knee deep in the ocean with a pair of
goggles on his face. He has a snorkel in his mouth. He has
his face down in the water looking at fish.

KATE AND MADDIE are lying on the beach watching FRANK.

                    MADDIE
          Oh dear, that monkey is going to
          drown himself Kate

                    KATE
          Don't be silly mom.

                    MADDIE
          You know monkeys can't swim.

                    KATE
          You wanna bet?

MADDIE looks at KATE.

                    MADDIE
          Yes. That ape will drown if he goes
          deeper.

                    KATE
          Stay here and watch.

KATE jumps up and wades into the water next to FRANK. She
takes his hand and leads him into deeper water. FRANK looks
up at KATE and follows her lead.

                    MADDIE
          Kate Beauregard, you will kill the
          captain's ape as sure as the world.
          That's enough, come back now.

KATE kneels down and puts her hands on FRANKS shoulders
pushing him down under the water. He disappears.

MADDIE jumps up from the beach towel (screaming)

                    MADDIE (cont'd)
          Oh dear God, she has drowned that
          poor ape! Please someone get them
          out of the water.

KATE dives down . FRANK is on her back smiling as she lifts
him out of the water. He paddles to shore (chattering).

                                              (CONTINUED)

Offshore, BUZZ KELLER is driving a jet ski with his wife
behind holding tight. The jet ski veers left then right
turning into the beach at full speed. The wife is thrown
headlong over BUZZ and onto the beach face first.

NADINE is watching the spectacle with JENELLA.

                    NADINE
          You would think they would figure
          out how to drive that thing by now.

                    JENELLA
          Do you think you could handle one
          of those jet skis?

                    NADINE
          Come on baby girl.

NADINE pays for a jet ski rental. She and JENELLA climb
aboard and take off. NADINE does donuts and figure eights at
full throttle. She takes off straight again and races over
waves launching the jet ski over each one. She turns back in
a hard 180 degree end swap and jets down the coast. JENELLA
(close up) . Eyes bulging.

NADINE drives the jet ski straight into the beach,
dismounts, helps JENELLA off the back and delivers the keys
to the pay shack. The vendor takes the keys.

NADINE escorts JENELLA back to the beach blankets and sits
down. She looks at JENELLA.

                    NADINE (cont'd)
          That's how it's done.

EXT BEACH. ROCKY LEDGE . SAME

BEN pulls JENNY up the rocky ledges as the ocean surf hits
the rocks. They reach the top and find a place to sit
together . JENNY is staring out to the horizon.BEN is
(STARING) at JENNY'S face.

                    BEN
               (whispers)
          What a beautiful sight.

                    JENNY
          Yes it is.

BEN (QUICKLY) turns away to look at the sea.

                         BEN
               Oh, yea. It is.

INT. BERTHA - NIGHT

MATT knocks on the SPARK'S cabin door. No answer. He knocks
again. The door is cracked open. Two eyes look at him.

                         ENRICO
               Who is it?

                         MATT
               Enrico?

                         ENRICO
               Si, Yes.

                         MATT
               I am the captain. Why don't you and
               I take a walk and get you out of
               here, OK?

                         ENRICO
               Mr. Jake said you would come for
               me.

                         MATT
               That's right son. Everything is
               alright. Just open the door and
               let's go have some fun.

ENRICO leaves with MATT.

EXT. PIER - SAME

Meat is grilling on the pier. KASEY HAYS is tuning the band.
Passengers are gathered near the impromptu stage. The sound
of laughter in the air. Children chasing each other across
the pier. The stars shine brightly in the night sky.

Two crewmen are busy setting up a fireworks display next to
BERTHA.

MATT and ENRICO move among the crowd and walk to a quiet
area under some palms.

                         MATT
               How would you like to work for me
               as a crewman on BERTHA?

                                           (CONTINUED)

                    ENRICO
          I would be honored to work for you
          captain.

                    MATT
          Alright, that is settled. You are
          now employed. I'll let the crew
          know. Now you go and have some fun
          with the Sparks family.

ENRICO walks away then turns, he raises his hand to MATT.

An open buffet serves the crowd. The band begins to play.
KASEY is singing. MATT spots KATE and moves toward her.

                    KATE
          What a great place to have a party.

                    MATT
          You know, these people deserve
          it.Are you hungry?

                    KATE
          Starving.

They disappear into the crowd.

JENELLA sees ENRICO .

                    JENELLA
          Hi.

                    ENRICO
          Hello.

                    JENELLA
          Why don't you sit with us over
          there. Are you hungry?

                    ENRICO
          Yes.

They move away from view.

Camera shows KASEY HAYS performing. People are dancing in
front of him. Smoke from the barbecue drifts across the
crowd.

KASEY finishes the song and reaches for the microphone.

                    KASEY
          Is everybody having a good time
          tonight?

Crowd (ROARS).

                    KASEY (cont'd)
          This song is dedicated to you folks
          and your captain. I hope you like
          it.

KASEY plays.

MATT and KATE join JOHN and MADDIE for dinner.

                    MADDIE
          Come sit with us.

                    JOHN
          MATT, this is some setup out here
          tonight.

                    MATT
          It sure is. Thanks to that man.

He points to KASEY.

                    JOHN
          Maybe so, but I am going to toast
          to you tonight.

JOHN raises a glass.

JAKE and family sit with ENRICO eating.

                    JAKE
          JJ, look they're setting up the
          fireworks over there.

JJ turns to look.

                    NADINE
          Rick,did you have a chance to talk
          to the captain?

                    ENRICO
          Yes mam, I am going to be his
          employee . This is a dream come
          true. I am excited about going to
          the United States.

                    JAKE
          You should be son. It is the best
          place a man could live. People just
          got to know how to appreciate it.

                    JENELLA
          Enrico, I mean Rick. Would you like
          to take a walk.

                    ENRICO
          Sure. Are you ready.

                    JENELLA
          Let's go.

ENRICO and JENELLA leave the table.

                    JAKE
          Oh boy. What is goin' on now.

                    NADINE
          Jake, you leave them two alone.

EXT. PIER LATER

KASEY holds the microphone.

                    KASEY
          Folks, if anyone wants to try
          singin', me and the boys will play
          behind you. Any takers out there?

ROY KELLER stands up slowly. He (SHUFFLES) slowly up to the
stage dressed in overalls and hat.

The crowd looks on.

                    KASEY (cont'd)
          How about that. Come on up sir.
          Give him a hand.

Crowd applauds .

ROY sits down on a stool in front of the microphone. KASEY
lowers the microphone in front of ROY.

                    KASEY (cont'd)
          Alright old timer, what is your
          name.

                    ROY
          My name is Roy Keller. People that
          knows me call me Buzz.

                    KASEY
          OK Buzz, what song have you got
          picked out.

                         ROY
          You probably don't know it. I don't
          need no helpa sangin' it.

                         KASEY
          Alright. It's all yours Buzz.

Kasey backs away.

Roy sits silently for a moment. He clears his throat and
adjusts his hat.

Roy begins singing in Accapella, OH DEATH, a song recorded
by Ralph Stanley.

The audience is still and silent. FRANK puts his hands over
his ears and shakes his head with his lips puckered.

ROY sings a few lines. The monotone (GRATES) the air. The
audience looks around.

                         KASEY (cont'd)
                    (INTERRUPTS)
          OK Buzz. We appreciate your singin.
          I think the fireworks is about to
          start. Everybody come back in a few
          minutes and we will play some more.

EXT. PIER . LATER

The sky lights up with brilliant explosions. Two crewmen are
lighting the fuses on the fireworks with lit cigars.

The crowd is looking up. The sound of thunder from the
explosions (echoes) across the harbor.

INT. BERTHA HULL. SAME

A crewman smoking a cigar opens a storage room door . Inside
are sticks of marine dynamite and fireworks. He picks up
several fireworks as the hot cinders of the cigar fall to
the floor. He switches off the light and shuts the door.

EXT. PIER. SAME

JAKE has him arm around NADINE as JJ sits near the front of
the crowd watching the display. MATT and KATE stand in the
rear watching.

A brilliant starburst firework illuminates the sky.

INT.BERTHA. HULL . SAME

The cigar cinders touch the tip of a clear wrapping paper
holding the marine dynamite. Smoke then fire begins.

EXT. PIER. SAME

Another series of explosions light up the sky. The sound of
(OOH) from the crowd.

A loud (BOOM) shakes BERTHA. Another (BOOM) comes from
within the boat. Fire shoots through the deck into the sky.
Another explosion (BOOM) blows the rear deck off into the
water.

The crowd runs away from BERTHA.

Fire erupts in the cabin superstructure . Billowing smoke
appears with leaping flames. Another (EXPLOSION). The
midsection of the cabin structure flies off into the water.
Fire and explosions continue.

MATT and KATE reach for passengers and pull them back. JAKE
looks for JENELLA and ENRICO as NADINE grabs JJ.

A scene of (PANIC) in the crowd as they move away.

MATT runs toward the boat. He grabs a crewman.

>   MATT
>   Is anybody on board!

>   CREWMAN
>   No sir, everybody is safe.

>   MATT
>   Are you sure?

>   CREWMAN
>   Yes sir.

>   MATT
>   OK. Go around and take a head
>   count.

MATT sees the Port Authority firetrucks coming down the
pier.

EXT. AIRPORT. ST. THOMAS - NEXT MORNING

MATT is standing beside a line of passengers in the airport
terminal. He has a cell phone to his ear.

                    MATT
          Yes sir. We have arranged for a
          flight to Mobile this morning. The
          hotel put us up for the night. I
          will talk to you when I get back.
          Goodbye.

MATT sees Kate with JOHN AND MADDIE. He walks over to them.

                    MATT (cont'd)
               (to JOHN)
          I just spoke with the banker and
          insurance company. The passenger
          liability is covered.

                    JOHN
          Good. Listen, don't be so hard on
          yourself. It was an accident.

                    MATT
          Maybe this whole trip was just one
          big accident.

                    KATE
          Matt, everyone is fine. You lost
          your boat. It is replaceable.

                    MATT
          Yea.

MIKE walks up.

                    MIKE
          We're ready to board. Keep your
          chin up. We'll do it again from
          scratch.

                    MATT
               (smile)
          Always the optimist.

INT. AIRPLANE - HOUR LATER

KATE is sitting with MATT. JOHN and MADDIE are sitting
behind them.

                         KATE
                      (to MATT)
               What are you reading?

MATT hands her a document. She reads it then looks at MATT
(INTENTLY).

                         KATE (cont'd)
               This is wonderful.

                         MATT
               Maybe so. I need to think about it.

                         KATE
               Can I share this with dad.

                         MATT
               Sure. Why not.

KATE reaches over the seat with the document.

                         KATE
               Dad, read this.

He takes the document and reads. MATT looks at Kate.

                         MATT
               You know, you look beautiful today.

                         KATE
               Thank you sir.

JOHN leans up . His face peers over the seats.

                         JOHN
               Matt, do you know what this means.

                         KATE
               Dad, he knows it is worth millions.

                         MATT
               Yes sir, it means a Cuban dictator
               wants me to bootleg whiskey. That
               would make me the biggest
               moonshiner in world history.

                         JOHN
               No. It means Cuba wants to buy
               corn, wheat and soy beans from you
               exclusively as a preferred trading
               partner. That is a business deal
               you can't afford to turn down.

                         MATT
          He also mentioned La Luna Brillante
          in bulk.

                         JOHN
          Corn bi- products.

                         MATT
               (pauses)
          I will need a bigger boat.

                         JOHN
          Place your order in Finland. In a
          year or so you will have your boat.

                         MATT
          I think this document will clear
          the way for the financing.

                         JOHN
          If you need a partner, I would be
          the first to jump on board.

                         MATT
          Thanks.

JAKE is sitting on an aisle seat with NADINE. Behind him
sits his golfing partner.

In the front of the plane a commotion of sound and a scream.
A stewardess is standing at the cockpit door. A man with a
weapon holds her from behind.

Nearer to JAKE in the aisle another man jumps up and grabs a
stewardess from behind holding something to her throat.

As the passengers look on, JAKE'S golfing partner leans
forward over the seat back close to JAKE'S ear.

                    GOLFING PARTNER
          Don't move.

JAKE (freezes)eyes wide.

A slingshot appears just above the top of JAKE'S seat. His
partner takes aim.(Whoosh)past JAKE'S ear flies a golf ball
hitting the would be hijacker between the eyes.

The hijacker drops (OUT COLD). The stewardess moves away
giving a view of the forward cabin.

Another volley flies down the aisle (SLOW MOTION)and hits
the second hijacker between the eyes. (OUT COLD).

The passengers (SHOUT)in unison.

EXT.MOBILE INTERNATIONAL AIRPORT - LATER

Two stretchers carry both hijackers off the plane into the
terminal. Both have large goose egg bumps on their
foreheads. They are moved away quickly out of sight.

The passengers then appear and enter the terminal. MATT is
walking with KATE.

A reporter approaches MATT.

                    REPORTER
          Captain sir, we understand one of
          your passengers has just thwarted
          an attempted hijacking. Can you
          comment.

                    MATT
          That was over before it started.
          Next question.

                    REPORTER
          Some people are calling BERTHA the
          redneck cruise ship. Any comment.

MADDIE is standing close by and moves toward the reporter.
She swings her purse at the cameraman.

                    MADDIE
          Those are fightin' words. Now ,
          leave him alone. Go away.

The reporter jumps back.

Passengers file by and leave the terminal area. MATT holds
KATE'S hand.

                    MATT
               (to Kate)
          Let's take a walk.

INT.CHURCH - 2 YEARS LATER. DAY

MOBILE, ALABAMA

View of an old country church with high beamed ceiling and
stained glass windows. A spectrum of light colors the church
sanctuary.

                                                  (CONTINUED)

JAKE is standing in a pew with his family. ENRICO is
standing next to JENELLA.

JAKE is looking forward . The camera pans to the alter.

MATT leans in to kiss KATE. They turn toward the
congregation. Loud (CHEERING) follows. The echoes cascade
through the large sanctuary.

Camera pans over to FRANK, dressed in a black tuxedo and
standing with MIKE. Both are smiling. (BROADLY)

The bride and groom move down the aisle past MADDIE AND
JOHN. They continue down the aisle passing all the
passengers from the cruise.

BEN stands next to JENNY . She is holding an infant.

At the doorway leading out of the church they turn looking
back. They wave at the attendees.

The church doors are opened.

Bright sunshine greets them as they walk out onto the deck
of BERTHA II, a Genesis cruise ship designed to accommodate
5,000 passengers.

MATT and KATE walk (BRISKLY) around the deck onto a
promenade walkway leading to the bridge elevator. FRANK
scampers to catch them.

Rice is thrown from all directions by thousands of
(APPLAUDING) passengers.

A view of MATT AND KATE entering a glass elevator . It
(ZOOMS) up to the bridge.

INT. CHURCH - SAME

JAKE and family are leaving the church. Someone hands JAKE
an envelope. He opens it and shows it to NADINE. Inside are
lifetime passes on BERTHA II. A check for $100,000
accompanies the tickets.

As the attendees pass by the front area of the church each
is handed an envelope.

JAKE looks at NADINE (SMILING).

EXT MOBILE BAY. SAME

BIRDSEYE VIEW

BERTHA II moves out to sea. On the forward and rear decks
large cargo hatches are imprinted with the word CORN.

THE END

FADE OUT